Jesse's Girl

By:

Brooke St. James

Other titles available from Brooke St. James:

Another Shot:
A Modern-Day Ruth and Boaz Story

When Lightning Strikes

Something of a Storm (All in Good Time #1)
Someone Someday (All in Good Time #2)

Finally My Forever (Meant for Me #1)
Finally My Heart's Desire (Meant for Me #2)
Finally My Happy Ending (Meant for Me #3)

Shot by Cupid's Arrow

Dreams of Us

Meet Me in Myrtle Beach (Hunt Family #1)
Kiss Me in Carolina (Hunt Family #2)
California's Calling (Hunt Family #3)
Back to the Beach (Hunt Family #4)
It's About Time (Hunt Family #5)

Loved Bayou (Martin Family #1)
Dear California (Martin Family #2)
My One Regret (Martin Family #3)
Broken and Beautiful (Martin Family #4)
Back to the Bayou (Martin Family #5)

Almost Christmas

JFK to Dublin (Shower & Shelter Artist Collective #1)
Not Your Average Joe (Shower & Shelter Artist Collective #2)
So Much for Boundaries (Shower & Shelter Artist Collective #3)
Suddenly Starstruck (Shower & Shelter Artist Collective #4)
Love Stung (Shower & Shelter Artist Collective #5)
My American Angel (Shower & Shelter Artist Collective #6)

Summer of '65 (Bishop Family #1)

3

Chapter 1

Rose Lewis
Memphis, TN
1989

Just about everyone in Memphis knew my family. If they didn't, they at least knew of us.

My grandfather, Dan Lewis, was the pastor of one of the largest churches in the city, and my father, Jacob, had followed in his footsteps, taking over the congregation when Pa retired.

Those who didn't know of my family through the church knew of us through my uncle's business. Over twenty-five years ago, my uncle by marriage, Michael Bishop, started Bishop Motorcycle Company, which was now a household name in the south (and quickly becoming one in the rest of the country).

Bishop Motorcycles had experienced staggering growth, but my Uncle Michael and Aunt Ivy were still very much a part of the day-to-day operation. As the business expanded, they bought the land around the original shop, and now there was a new garage and showroom with an attached office wing and parts-plant. Bishop Motorcycles now had over a hundred employees.

Seeing as how my dad, Jacob, was Ivy's little brother, he had been working and hanging out at the motorcycle shop since its humble beginnings at Mr. Morrow's body shop. My dad loved being there, and he especially loved helping out in the garage and getting his hands dirty after a week of pastoral duties. My mom was one of Aunt Ivy's best friends, and I was close in age to my twin cousins, so our families spent a lot of time together when I was a young.

During my early childhood, Aunt Ivy had a successful music career as a blues and soul singer. I can remember her going on tour every summer. Uncle Michael would stay home to run the business, and Aunt Ivy would schedule all of her concerts during the summer so she could take my cousins with her after they finished school. I hated this part of the year because I loved my cousins and hated to see them go.

Jesse and Jane were both talented musically, so it was a natural progression that they began to go on stage with their mom. *What's cuter than a twin, brother-sister act with kids who were actually talented, after all?* Eventually, Jesse and Jane became the opening act for Ivy and played a few of songs with her during her set.

This summer tour tradition went on until Ivy decided to stay home to help Michael with the business full-time. Both Jesse and Jane were talented and could have pursued careers in music, but they were becoming teenagers by the time Ivy quit touring, and they had other interests that ultimately conflicted with doing music.

So there was my family in a nutshell—pastors, musicians, and motorcycles. Sure, it might be a little unorthodox for a pastor to spend his spare time in a motorcycle shop, but nothing had ever really been ordinary in my father's life.

The Lewis family had adopted my father when he appeared on their doorstep, swaddled and lying in a basket like Moses. When my parents and grandparents tell the story, they say that the Lewis's probably would have named him Moses if there hadn't been a note in the basket requesting that they call him Jacob.

That story always made people picture my dad being found on a doorstep in a nice, bassinette-type basket that was very stable with plenty of room, but that couldn't be further from the truth. Dad's basket was a small, worn out, cheaply made Easter basket.

My grandma had told me that version one day when I was complaining about my dad. She said it was a wonder the basket held together. It was a real miracle he had made it safely into her arms instead of rolling down the steps. That wasn't where my dad's miracle stopped, either. Vicki and Dan Lewis (in spite of being very white by race and living in a time of more heated race relations) adopted my dad who was quite a bit darker than them. No one knew my dad's real heritage. He was light-skinned for a black man but too dark to be white or even Spanish.

My mother, Alice Adams, on the other hand, was as white as they come—she came complete with blonde hair and blue eyes, looking like she was straight from the European countryside. My little brothers got my dad's dark hair and eyes, but I ended up with lighter eyes and hair like my mom and a skin tone that fell somewhere between my mom's and dad's.

My mom and Aunt Ivy had been good friends since they were kids. My dad had a crush on my mom his whole life, but he was always too shy to tell her. He finally professed his love right before he left for seminary, and the rest, as they say, is history. In spite of being five years older than him, my mom returned the sentiment, and she and my dad got married before he left for school in Kentucky.

She found out she was pregnant with me soon after they were married, and they spent the next four years being starving students and doing their best to raise me without the help of family nearby. They laugh about how poor they were during those years, but they must have been a pretty good team, because all of my childhood memories are peaceful ones, and the pictures I've seen of my baby days portray my parents being happy and content.

Dad was so young when they had me, that he and my mom waited six years before having another child. I now have two younger brothers who were born back-to-back after Mom and Dad got settled back home in Memphis. My brothers were so much younger than me that, in some ways, I felt as though I was an only child. I spent much of my adolescence tagging along with Dad while Mom was busy at home with the boys.

The boys were teenagers now, and I was currently finishing up my junior year of college.

My parents' house (the church parsonage) wasn't built for a family of five, so I had long-since moved out. I had been living on my own for the last three years despite the fact that I went to college right there in Memphis and could have easily stayed at home. My parents did what they could to support me financially, but both of my brothers were competitive in multiple sports, and they had a lot of expenses with that. They lived a modest lifestyle to try to provide for us kids, so it was pretty early on that I started doing what I could to help out and pay my own way.

I had a small apartment near the university that I shared with my friend, Rebecca.

I worked on campus and went to college full-time, so I rarely strayed too far unless I was going to my parents' house to eat or do laundry.

I was studying mathematics with an emphasis on statistics. I was now and had always been a numbers girl. Numbers made sense to me. I loved mathematics because there were concrete rules with consistent results. I had a special affinity for statistics and could stare at graphs and charts all day without getting bored. I worked at the University Credit Union as a teller while I was studying, but seeing as how my real passion was analyzing statistics, I had recently made it my goal to become self-employed.

It was something I knew I could be good at.

My plan was to study a business mathematically and translate my findings into practical marketing advice. I had done similar projects in school and thought I had a successful business model. I liked math and I liked working with people, so this idea seemed like a perfect fit. I needed experience with a real business, though.

It was for this reason that I was sitting in Uncle Michael's office, staring at him from across his oversized wooden desk. It was the same desk he had in the other location, and I remembered playing underneath it when I was little. He had a recent family picture on it, and I stared at it, thinking that my cousin, Jesse, was perhaps the most incredible male specimen I had ever seen. I had always loved the way Jesse looked, and he had only gotten more and more handsome as we got older.

Uncle Michael shifted the paperwork on his desk, drawing me back from my thoughts. He smiled proudly. "This is really something, Rose," he said, sitting back in his chair with a piece of paper in his hand.

He stared at it again for a few long seconds while my heart pounded. I felt terrified in spite of the fact that I was offering my services for free. I had been anxious that he might still turn me down. I wondered if maybe he would just think it was a bad idea and say 'no thanks'.

Uncle Michael finally looked at me again after he stared at the paper. "This is gonna be a lot of work," he said. "I certainly wouldn't expect you to do this for free, sweetheart."

I smiled with relief that he wanted me to do it at all. "It would *help* me," I assured him. "If I do yours for free and it works out, I get to charge the next person. I was talking to my professor about the idea, and he said I'd learn a lot during my first attempt, warning me that I'd need to work out the kinks with my process. You'd be doing me a favor to let me use your company to blaze a trail for myself. I'd really be honored."

He crossed his arms in front of his chest and smiled at me with the type of proud smile that made me feel like he was thinking my parents had done a good job raising me or something else warm and fuzzy like that.

"I'd be honored to be your first client, Rose," he said. "But I have terms."

"Yes sir. What are they?" I asked, sitting up, ready to take notes.

He smiled. "We'll look at the marketing strategies you recommend. If we decide to try them, and our revenues go up, I'll pay you twenty percent of our increase for the first three months."

My heart started racing as I thought of all the possibilities. I really thought I could increase his revenue, and I couldn't help but start doing some of the math in my head.

"Twenty's too much," I said. I shrugged. "I like the idea of getting some small percentage of the increase because that makes it even more of a challenge for me, but twenty's way too much."

Michael smiled and tilted his head at me. "The way I look at it, the increase doesn't exist without you. So, it's more like *you're* offering *me eighty* percent rather than me offering you twenty."

He was right and I knew it. It was with a pounding heart and a huge smile that I stuck out my hand to shake his. "Deal," I said. "I'm about to get rich," I added, making him laugh. I stood and started gathering up the paperwork that was on his desk.

"You're a smart girl, Rose," he said sweetly. "I'm proud of you for coming up with all this."

I glanced at him with a smile. "Thank you."

"Thank you," he said. "I'm excited to see what you come up with."

"Me too. It's gonna be fun."

"You can have access to whatever you need," he said.

I nodded. "Thank you. It'll help me to have access to your books from the last few years. I'll talk to the accountant. I'm anticipating that my first attempt at this will take longer than any of the others, but I have no idea what kind of timeframe to give you." I shrugged. "Maybe a month or two. I hope I'm not going to be in anybody's way if I come up here some during that time."

"Are you kidding? We *want* you around the shop. You've been coming around way too little since you grew up." He smiled at me. "I wish you'd come to work for me in the showroom. That's marketing with no statistical research or effort whatsoever."

I smiled. "I'll take that as a compliment," I said.

"You should," he said. "It was one. You've always been a beautiful young lady, Rose."

He came around the desk to give me a hug, and I smiled at him.

"Thank you," I said.

He patted my shoulder in a gesture that said *you're welcome*. "Are you still dating the basketball player?" he asked.

I nodded. Everyone knew Barrett as 'the basketball player' because he was 6' 9" and one of the MVP's on the college basketball team. He was a year older than me and was just wrapping up his senior-year basketball season, which had been a huge success.

"Yes sir," I said. "He's got two more games this year, but they're both away. I'm gonna miss going to them once he's all done."

"Last time he was with you at Nana & Pa's, I heard him tell your dad he was going into the NBA."

I smiled and shrugged. "He's hoping to get drafted this summer," I said. "I think he's got a decent chance—that seems to be the word, anyway."

"That's exciting," he said.

I nodded as we headed toward the door. "Yes sir it is." I gestured to my paperwork. "I'm excited about getting with this, too."

"Me too," he said. "Thank you."

"I'll get started next week if that's okay."

"Sounds perfect," he said. He patted my back as we walked across his office and started down the hall. "I'll walk you out."

I had come by after I got off work at the bank, so it was afterhours and the place was really quiet. Uncle Michael must have thought I parked in the back, because he led me towards the garage rather than out the office doors. I didn't mind walking through the shop, so I didn't tell him any different. There were still a few people making noise and closing up, but it was Friday evening, so most everyone had clocked out and gone home for the day.

We were walking down the hall and had almost reached the door to the shop when I heard the sound of a siren. It gave three shrill calls matching the tone

13

of a police siren, and then I heard, "Intruder alert! Intruder alert!" in the high-pitched voice of what was obviously a talking bird. There were three more siren calls, and I looked at my uncle and rolled my eyes as we opened the door to the shop.

"Is Elvis your security system?" I asked.

He smiled and shook his head. "Hardly. That's just what he says when he sees Jesse."

Chapter 2

I had come in through the office entrance, so I had completely forgotten about Elvis—a flashy blue and gold Macaw with an extensive vocabulary. He had belonged to Mr. Morrow, the man who owned the garage before Michael. Mr. Morrow kept the bird in his body shop, and when he died and left the shop to Michael, his children re-homed the bird.

Elvis slowly took a turn for the worse, becoming lethargic and pulling out his own feathers. This didn't stop until two years later when Mr. Morrow's son, Buddy, called Michael and asked if he would be interested in letting him live in the garage again. Michael agreed, and here we were, twenty something years later with Elvis the still at the shop.

"He's the shop mascot, isn't he?" I said as we walked more fully into the garage.

He smiled at my question, and then I watched as his smile broadened at whatever caught his attention. "I knew you were here," Uncle Michael said.

I glanced that way to find Jesse Bishop standing there, smiling at both of us. He was dressed so nicely that I knew he wasn't there to work. He looked so handsome that I instinctually straightened my posture. Jesse was just like his dad when it came to a love for building motorcycles, and he was usually up to his elbows in grime and grease. I could hardly look at him when he was all clean-shaven and sharp-looking.

"What's she doing here?" Jesse asked, talking to his dad but staring straight at me.

"She's gonna be working here for a couple of months."

"Working here?" Jesse asked, surprised.

"Office stuff," I said. "Marketing research. Your dad's letting me try out some ideas."

Jesse shrugged a little as he crossed the space between us, reaching out to give me a casual hug. We were on the side of the garage with most of the workspace expanding out toward my left. There were a couple of people on the other side of the room, but they were too far from us to hear what we were saying. Elvis has become preoccupied with something near his perch and was now bobbing up and down and looking in the other direction.

"I can't believe my dad finally talked you into coming to work for us," Jesse said, looking at me with his arm still around my shoulder.

"Looks like you're all spiffied-up," I said, breathing in his clean, masculine smell as he hugged me.

"I even scrubbed under my fingernails," he said. He thrust his big hand in front of me as if I should see for myself. I reached out for it and gave it a thorough inspection, turning it over and noticing that his nails were indeed grease free.

I tried my best to ignore the nervous feeling I got from touching him. I glanced up, and we made eye contact. He had light green eyes—the most beautiful eyes that had ever been put in a human being. Jesse's eyes. I was convinced he had the only pair like them in the world. He wasn't as tall as my boyfriend, but he was thicker.

I still had his hand in mine when Elvis made the sound of a doorbell and said, "Come on in!" indicating that someone had just come in the main door.

"Everyone else gets a nice greeting," Uncle Michael said with a smile. "Except for Jesse, he gets sirens. Uncle Max taught him that."

I was laughing at that and hadn't even seen who came in the door, but then I heard a woman's voice.

"I thought you were just coming in to get your glasses," she said. I turned to find Tammy Gwinn standing there, looking straight at Jesse with a wide-eyed, in-a-hurry expression. "Where are your glasses?" she asked.

"Hey Tammy," Uncle Michael said.

"Hi," she said, smiling at Michael and then quickly at me before looking at Jesse again. When she first glanced at me, she looked annoyed by my proximity to Jesse, but she recognized me quickly. We had met each other a few times before, and she knew I was Jesse's cousin.

"We've got a wedding to go to," she said with another rushed expression aimed at Jesse.

He walked over to his workstation in search of his glasses. "She's a bridesmaid," he said as if to explain his girlfriend's fussy behavior. He took a pair of wire-framed glasses off of the counter and put them on his face, adjusting them before focusing on us again. Tammy had come into the room by this time, and I turned to find her standing in her lavender colored, satin, floor-length dress. Her blonde hair was teased to perfection and sealed to an indestructible finish with about a can of hairspray. I knew her as Jesse's girlfriend, but I also knew her as the head cheerleader at UM. I went to all of Barrett's games, so I saw Tammy and her cheerleading squad on a regular basis.

"I got some dust in my eyes from the polisher today, and my contacts were bothering me," Jesse explained, coming to stand near us again.

"You ready?" Tammy asked with no regard to his comment.

He nodded and went to stand next to her.

My heart broke. I wasn't a woman-hater, but I did not like Tammy Gwinn, and I didn't want my cousin to like her either. I didn't know what he saw in her other than a perfect exterior.

"I'm glad you're coming to work here," Jesse said, smiling at me as he started to pull his girlfriend toward the door.

"You're coming to work here?" Tammy asked, glancing at me with newfound curiosity.

"Short term," I said with a shrug. "Office stuff. Marketing analysis."

"Oh, that's right, you're a math and science person."

A nerd. That's what she was thinking. I could see it in her condescending smile. Everyone else in the room thought her smile was totally genuine, so I pretended I thought so too and gave her a fake but genuine-looking one of my own.

"We should get together sometime," she said, surprising me. "You're dating Barrett Hall, right?"

I nodded and she smiled. "I love Barrett," she said. "I hang out with all those guys." She glanced at Jesse. "We should all get together sometime."

Jesse shrugged at me, and I gave him a skeptical expression, which I changed to a smile as soon as Tammy faced me again.

"Sure," I said. "Maybe once the season is over and I get through my finals."

She smiled and shrugged before motioning to Jesse.

"Bye, y'all," Jesse said.

"Bye y'all!" Elvis called loudly. "Y'all come back!" he added as they let the door close behind them.

I smiled at my uncle and shook my head at the bird. I wanted to say something about how annoying Tammy was now that they were gone, but Uncle Michael was smiling and didn't seem annoyed at all, so I kept my comments to myself.

19

"Thank you," I said, hugging him. "I'm excited to get started."

He squeezed me tightly. "Thank you, Rose. I'm excited, too."

He held open the door for me, not knowing that I had to walk around the building to get to my car.

***

My roommate, Rebecca, was sitting in the living room when I got back to my apartment.

"Barrett called," was the first thing she said when I walked in the door. "How'd it go?" she added as I kicked off my shoes.

I smiled. "Good. I got the job."

She clapped and whooped for me, and I was still smiling about that as I crossed to the kitchen. Our small apartment had a peninsula separating the kitchen and living room, and I sat on one of the barstools, looking at Rebecca.

"*And* he's gonna pay me," I said.

"He is? How much?" she asked.

"Commission, I think. He was saying something about me taking a percentage, but I don't know. We'll have to talk about it." I stared at the wall behind Rebecca and said the words in a slow, dazed tone because I could not stop thinking about Jesse. I thought I had gotten the encounter with him out of my head, and I felt annoyed and agitated with myself that my thoughts kept going back to him.

I breathed a sigh, reminding myself to focus on the conversation with Rebecca, and she took it as a

20

sigh of disappointment. She looked at me with a perplexed expression. "What's wrong? I thought you'd be happy about getting paid. I thought you were planning on doing it for free."

I smiled. "Nothing," I said. "It wasn't that. It was just a tired sigh." I swiveled in the barstool. "I'm going to take a shower."

"Aren't you gonna call Barrett back?" she asked.

I glanced at the kitchen phone that was hanging on the wall right next to us. "I think I'm gonna take a shower first," I said. "If he calls again, just tell him I'll call him back in a few minutes."

"You okay?" she asked as I began walking backward toward my bedroom.

"Yeah."

"Do you still want to go see a movie?"

"Yeah, why?" I asked.

She shrugged. "I don't know I just thought you looked upset for a second."

I shook my head. "Just tired," I said.

I didn't even need a shower. In fact, I was making more work for myself by taking one. I had plans to go to the movies with Rebecca that evening, and a shower just meant that I'd have to get dressed again. I didn't, however, see how I had any other choice. I had to do it in order to shock the thought of Jesse Bishop right out of my head.

When I was a little girl, I had a friend named Phillip who told me that when I got sad about something, all I had to do was take an ice cold

21

shower, and it would wash the feelings away. The colder the shower, the better the affects. I was generally a happy person, but I had taken anywhere from thirty to fifty of these ice cold showers in my lifetime. None of them had ever fully worked to get rid of whatever was bothering me, but I still did it every time I felt overwhelmed just in case.

I started the shower running warm water just to ease myself into it. I stepped in and let the water run all over my face and hair, feeling like I wanted to cry over my lot in life but not letting myself. Technically, I had a productive day with the job and everything, but Jesse.

Jesse.

I knew there was a chance that I would run into him once I started working at my uncle's place, but I certainly hadn't expected to see him today.

He was the most wonderful man—the man of my dreams. He was smart, handsome, rugged, and athletic, and yet humble and tender.

Jesse Bishop.

He was all of these perfect, wonderful things, but he was also...

my first cousin.

I felt miserable as I let the water wash over me. I had been madly in love with Jesse for most of my life, and I hated myself for it.

A flood of memories hit me. The first was a conversation I had with a girl named Emily when I was in the second grade. She was older than me and had been cluing me in on the idea of boys and relationships and crushes. She asked me if I liked any boy, and I told her I liked Jesse, at which point she grimaced and told me that was disgusting and a first-class sin to marry your cousin or to even be attracted to him in any way. She gave me a lecture about it and told me I could never, ever think that way about Jesse again. She said *she* could think that way about Jesse because she wasn't his cousin, but I clearly couldn't.

Emily scared me to death that day, but she assured me she wouldn't tell anybody about what I said, which made me feel a little better. I still lost sleep over it.

I put Jesse out of my mind for years after that. I was around him all the time, but I had assured myself that I could never have feelings for him.

I learned somewhere during my adolescence that he wasn't really blood related to me at all, but that didn't matter since everyone (including Jesse) just thought of us as cousins.

I was able to keep my distance and keep him out of my thoughts until one dreaded night when I was fifteen.

Chapter 3

My worst-ever Jesse relapse happened the night we watched the video of Michael Jackson's Thriller. I was a freshman in high school, and Jesse was a junior. There was a huge group of us at a friend's house. His name was Chris Hanks, and he had a big screen TV, which was a huge deal.

Chris and his family had a mansion with lots of property, and we all watched the Thriller video before going out to a bonfire in his backyard. Most of our high school was there, so I didn't even talk to Jesse until later that night when a lot of people had already gone home. Jesse was staying the night at Chris's, and I was riding home with someone who was staying late, so we were two of the remaining ten or twelve at the end of the night.

It was during that time when I left the garage and went to the bonfire. I found Jesse there. He was sitting on a log, poking at the fire with a huge stick—probably six or eight feet in length. It had to be that long because the fire was huge and hot, and he couldn't get any closer.

Two other people were sitting nearby, but they were preoccupied with each other, so I only spared them a quick glance before looking at Jesse again. He smiled at me, and my heart melted just like it did every time. I smiled back and waved, trying to look unruffled.

I was just about to sit on the opposite side of the bonfire, but Jesse patted the seat next to him, indicating that I should go over there. I could hear music playing from the garage. It was pop radio, and they were playing a song Jesse knew by heart, so he unabashedly sang it out.

He was being silly and smiling the whole time, but he had undeniable musical talent. I was dreading being next to him even before I sat down. I initially left three feet of space between us, and Jesse stared down at the empty space and then at me with a questioning expression.

"What's the matter? You don't like my singin'?"

I smiled and scooted slightly closer. "I love your singin'," I said. "I just didn't want to get too close while you were stirring up the fire."

He smiled at me, and then I watched as the look on his face shifted. He grew gravely serious, staring at me with a predatory expression. He scooted close to me, puffing out his chest, breathing deeply, and staring down at me in the most intimidating way possible.

"Were you scared from that Thriller video?" he asked, trying to scare me.

"I wasn't too scared," I said in a damsel in distress type voice with a hand to my chest, mimicking the actual video as much as I could.

Jesse held his serious expression and puffed out his chest even more as if to say that I was a fool for not being afraid.

"Maybe you *should have been scared*," he said, still looking deadly serious as he stared straight at me. He had always been a bit of an actor, so it made sense that he was trying to convince me that he was a zombie or whatever Michael Jackson was in the video.

What did surprise me was the way he continued looking at me. Jesse was messing around for the first few seconds, but I watched in amazement as his expression shifted from one of *crazed-zombie* to one of curiosity, or confusion, or frustration, or some mixture of all three. Jesse took a deep breath, and I watched his chest rise and fall as he continued to stare at me. He looked at my whole face, stopping to stare at my mouth, and for about five glorious seconds, I thought Jesse Bishop, the love of my life, was actually going to *kiss me*. I knew in my heart that he wanted to—I could see it by the way he looked at me. He stared at me for what seemed like forever before he finally broke eye contact.

"Your dad was adopted, anyway," he said in a frustrated mumbling tone as he turned to poke at the fire again.

"What?" I asked. My fifteen-year-old heart was about to pound out of my chest. "What'd you say?" I asked.

"Nothing," he said. "I was just messing around with you." He shrugged it off and turned to say something to Jason, the guy who was sitting close by with his girlfriend.

That night did me in for quite sometime. Nothing ever happened between us, but the memory of the way Jesse looked at me that night stayed with me for way longer than I cared to admit.

Okay, I'll admit it.

Two years.

I didn't completely obsess about him for that long, but I didn't date anyone else either. It wasn't that I was hopelessly devoted to Jesse as much as it was the simple fact that no one else was as good as him. I compared all potential suitors to him, and they all fell short.

Barrett was the first guy I felt a real attraction to, and that wasn't until my sophomore year of college. I dated a few guys off-and-on for very short periods of time during high school and my first year of college, but Barrett was my first long-term boyfriend. I had been with him for a little over a year now, and thought things were going pretty well—until I saw Jesse at the shop.

I was close to my family, and Jesse's sister, Jane, was one of my best friends, but I really only saw Jesse at family occasions, and there were always a lot of people around, so it was easy for me to act busy and not pay much attention to him.

But not tonight.

Tonight there was a hug.

I replayed the whole scene in my mind... the way he hugged me while I held his hand, searching for non-existent dirt under his fingernails. He was always easy to hug, and I could have been in that position a lot over the years, but I had somehow always managed to evade him.

If he had been my blood relative, it would have been easy for my heart to understand that he was off-limits, but as it stood, my brain said no but my heart still rebelled. I was drawn to Jesse the way you're drawn to a famous movie star—hopelessly and perpetually crushing even though you know you'll never have them.

I remembered the way he smiled and put on his glasses. I remembered thinking what a juxtaposition it was that this tough, motorcycle-building guy could be so sweet and adorable.

I felt my stomach tie into knots when I thought of Tammy in her lavender dress, beckoning Jesse to come over there and telling him to hurry up. I felt hot blood rush to my face at the memory of it, and I reached down to adjust the faucet.

I twisted the knob all the way to the right and gasped when my shower switched from pleasant to shockingly cold. I gasped two or three times as I did my best to get used to the cold water. If nothing else, the miserable shock of it served to distract me for a minute.

I went to my bedroom a few minutes later, feeling a little better.

"Barrett called again!" I heard Rebecca's muffled voice as she yelled through the walls.

"Thanks!" I yelled back.

My little brothers had gotten me a Swatch phone for Christmas. It was the kind where two people could use it at once. One person would use the receiver, and the other could pick up the base and use it has a second receiver. My brothers thought it was the coolest thing, and it really was, only I never found myself in a situation where I wanted to let someone listen-in on my phone calls. It was a neat looking phone, though, and I picked up the teal and pink receiver and dialed Barrett's number.

He picked up on the second ring.

"Hello," he said.

"Hey."

"What are you doing?" he asked.

"I just got out of the shower, why?"

"I was gonna come by and pick you up to come to a wedding with me."

"Why are you still in town?" I asked. "I thought y'all were leaving for the game."

"Something happened with the bus. It's only a three-hour drive, so coach said we'll just leave in the morning. Everybody's going to the wedding now. I was gonna see if you wanted to come with me."

"What wedding? I was planning on seeing a movie with Rebecca."

"You can do that anytime. Randall Boyd only gets married once, and it's tonight. Everybody's gonna be there. Most of the team's going to the reception. We're gonna surprise him."

Randall Boyd graduated two years earlier. He was the star center for the Tiger basketball team and a beloved Memphis athlete. There was no doubt in my mind that Tammy was a bridesmaid and Jesse was a guest at this very same wedding.

I couldn't see him again so soon.

"A wedding reception?" I asked in a tone that very clearly meant I did not want to go. "Why don't you just come to the movies with me and Rebecca?"

"Because I don't want to," Barrett said. "Everybody's going to that party."

"I wasn't invited to that," I said. I had a towel wrapped around my head, but I took it down, letting my damp hair fall onto my shoulders. I ran my fingers through it, not even caring that there were tangles.

"I *was* invited," Barrett said. "The whole team was. Randall's our homeboy. We just didn't think we'd get to go because of the game."

"Y'all still have a game tomorrow," I said. "You don't need to go out partying all night."

He breathed a laugh. "It's a wedding, Rose—not a bachelor party. We're not even going to the wedding, just the reception. I want to go. Me and Randall are tight. You don't have to come if you don't want to, but I'm going."

"I hate to do that to Rebecca," I said.

"Tell her to come," he said. "Nobody will care. We're showing up with a group, anyway. Plus, it's supposed to be huge."

There was a long period of silence where I contemplated whether or not I wanted to see Jesse.

"Or not," Barrett said when I hesitated.

"I'll go," I said. "We'll go. If you're sure nobody's gonna care that we weren't invited."

"You're invited," he said. "We're invited. I already told you that. All the guys are going and taking their girlfriends."

"What time?" I asked. I felt suddenly nervous and anxious as the reality of the change of plans set in.

"I'll pick you up at eight."

I glanced at the digital clock by my bed, which read 6:49. "Okay, we'll be ready."

"All right, see you in a few," he said.

We told each other goodbye, and I hung up the phone before going into the other room to talk to Rebecca. She liked Barrett and easily agreed to change plans so that I could hang out with him.

She and I turned on the radio and spent the next hour getting ready. We were both in good moods and had been singing along with every song that came on. The station we were listening to played pop hits, so it didn't surprise me when a song called *Jessie's Girl* came on. I tried to contain my enthusiasm when it started, but I loved the sound of the song so much that I just couldn't help myself. That familiar guitar lick was just too catchy.

Instead of turning the radio off, I reached down and turned it up, shaking my hips to the beat.

Rebecca was still putting the finishing touches on her hair with a curling iron, but I was done getting dressed. In spite of knowing it was wrong, I felt happy at the prospect of seeing my cousin again. I was in a good mood because of it, and I reached out for a nearby hairbrush and held it to my mouth like a microphone.

The song was in a comfortable key for me, so I sang the words I knew so well.

Jesse is a friend.
Yeah, I know he's been a good friend of mine.
But lately something's changed that ain't hard to define,
Jesse's got himself a girl, and I really don't know why.
And she's watching him with those eyes,
And she's loving him with that body, I just know it.
Yeah 'n' he's holding her in his arms late, late at night.
You know I wish that I was Jesse's girl.
I wish that I was Jesse's girl.
Why does he want a woman like that?

I thought I had been doing a good job of staying on pitch, so it surprised me when I opened my eyes to find my roommate staring at me with a dumbfounded expression.

"What?" I asked, as the song continued without me.

"You changed the lyrics," she said.

"No I didn't."

"You sure did. You were singing totally different words than him."

I had been singing the song with those modified lyrics for so long that I didn't even remember that they were modified.

"That's because he's a *guy* singing and a girl can't sing that song with those words, so I changed it. He just said 'moot'," I added out of nowhere when I heard Rick Springfield say the word in the song.

"What?" Rebecca asked looking even more confused.

"Moot," I said. "What kind of word is that? It sounds so weird."

"What are you talking about?" she asked.

I pointed at the stereo. "The song," I said. "There's a line in the song that says *the point is probably moot*. I know it's a real word; I just don't like it. I've literally never said it in a conversation. I think it makes me feel like he's trying to say the word *mute* and he's mispronouncing it—or maybe even a mote, like the thing around a castle. It's just an odd-sounding word, don't you think?"

Rebecca stared at me with a thoughtful expression. I couldn't tell if she thought I was crazy or if she was contemplating how she felt about the word moot.

"I don't think I've ever used that word either," she said. "I didn't even realize he said that in the song."

I nodded. "He said, *'I want to tell him that I love him, but the point is probably moot'.* What kind of word is *moot*, anyway?"

"See, you did it again," Rebecca said.

"Did what?"

"Changed the words," she said.

"Huh," I huffed, sounding surprised at myself. "I guess I just change the *hers* to *him* since I'm a girl," I said casually.

I tossed the hairbrush onto my bed and turned down the radio so I didn't get myself into more trouble.

Chapter 4

Barrett was a few minutes late picking Rebecca and me up for the wedding. He had called me while we were getting dressed to say that we would be riding with his friend, Tyler. Tyler was famous for being late, so it was kind of like they were right on time when they showed up fifteen minutes behind schedule.

I sat in the backseat with Barrett, feeling thankful that I had a dashing escort for the evening but still unable to fully stop thinking about Jesse. My mind would be completely off of him, and then somehow it would float back.

I couldn't help but wonder if I would see him or talk to him at the wedding, and I imagined different scenarios and possible conversations we might have. There were seven of us riding in Tyler's Suburban, so there was always something being said to draw me from my thoughts.

Before I knew it, we had arrived at the country club. We got out at the front, and after Tyler took care of talking to the valet, we headed for the door.

I had one dress that was formal enough for a wedding, so that's what I wore. I had light hazel eyes and the dress, which was blue, brought out the green in them. I had worn it a few other times and always got compliments. It was my best shot at confidence, so it was the one I chose. I always wore high heels when I went out with Barrett on account of his height, and tonight I wore my favorite pair.

Barrett kept his hand on me from the moment we got out of the vehicle. He wasn't being rude or inappropriate, and it wasn't that uncommon for him to make contact with me in public, but tonight it bothered me for other reasons. I tried not to make it too obvious but I did create some slight distance between Barrett and myself.

There was a live band playing and a huge dance floor. A big group was already out there slow dancing to a rock ballad when we arrived. It was much more of a party atmosphere than I imagined. I didn't have much experience with country clubs, but when Barrett said this reception was at one of them, I assumed it would be really subdued. I thought we'd be having tea and crumpets with our pinkies lifted high in the air, but instead, there was a band playing *I'll be There for You* by Bon Jovi. It was like a school dance, only fancier and with free drinks and buffet.

Barrett knew everyone.

Many of the wedding guests were tied into Memphis basketball, and he was one of the current star players, so he was a real hit at the party. Randall was so glad to have the guys from the team there, that he made an announcement wishing them good luck on their game the following day and teasing them about sabotaging the bus so that they could come to the wedding. He had the whole team come out onto the dance floor so that the photographer could get a picture of them together.

One of the more vocal guys on the team, the point guard named Derek Miller, said a few words from the team about Randall, commenting on how influential he had been and congratulating him on his wedding. He made a sweet, funny speech from the team.

The guys were still taking pictures at the edge of the dance floor when I felt a finger touch my shoulder.

I turned, and there he was.

Jesse.

We had been there almost an hour and I had already seen him, but not up close. I had been trying to avoid him, if you wanted to know the truth, because seeing him did nothing but remind me why I'd been choosing to avoid him all these years.

"Twice in one day," he said, reading my mind as he came in for a sideways hug.

I hugged him back, taking a calming breath. "I know," I said. I gestured toward the dance floor at the basketball players who were huddled together, taking a picture. There were several cheerleaders present, and they were all trying to get in on the action.

"The whole team decided to come last minute," I said to Jesse as we both stood there looking at them.

"You're still with that guy," Jesse said as more of a observation.

"You're still with that girl," I said.

My tone was slightly more serious than I intended, and it caused Jesse to glance at me curiously.

"No, she's great," I said. "She's really pretty."

"Yeah."

"I saw Jane yesterday," I said.

I saw Jesse's twin sister on a regular basis. She was a single mom with a three-year-old girl, and I loved her and her daughter dearly. I kept little Shelby twice a month on Thursday evenings while Jane went to band practice.

"She said you keep Shelby for her sometimes," Jesse said.

I nodded. "She's getting so big."

"Thank you for doing that," he said.

"It's my pleasure. I'm glad I get to see Shelby regularly. She's such a little sweetheart."

Jesse and I stood there for a few seconds, still watching the action on the dance floor. The band had started playing again, so now there were people dancing while photos were being taken.

"I didn't know you were coming to work at the company," Jesse said from next to me.

I could feel him looking at the side of my face, and I knew it would be awkward for me to avoid eye contact even though looking at him was dangerous. I glanced at him, almost cringing at how very attractive he was. I was so dazed by his appearance that I almost forgot it was my turn to talk.

I smiled. "I'm so thankful your dad's letting me do it," I said.

"What exactly are you doing?" he asked.

"Basically a lot of research and math. But hopefully it'll translate into you guys selling more motorcycles. That's the idea."

"I know we're always interested in doing that," Jesse said. "I'm just surprised dad didn't let me know he was hiring you."

"He wasn't," I said. "He isn't. He didn't come to me; I went to him. I didn't even tell him what I wanted to talk to him about when I asked him if I could come by the shop. I basically showed up there and told him these big ideas I had, asking if I could use your company as a guinea pig."

"So, you're not gonna be back in the garage building bikes?" he asked with a smile.

I smiled back and shook my head. "No bike-building for me," I said.

I had to look away.

Just being near him made me have a vision of the following thing:

Jesse, right there in that very moment at the wedding, would stare at me with great earnestness and say, *"We're not cousins, Rose. We're not related at all. What are we doing wasting our time being with other people when we're meant to be together? I love you. Will you marry me?"*

I took a deep breath, focusing my attention on the dance floor again. Jesse was standing right next to me, both of us looking straight ahead. My eye fell on Tammy who was giggling with her friends and posing for photographs. "I don't care for your girlfriend," I said.

The statement was already out of my mouth by the time I realized it was a rude thing for me to say.

"That makes two of us," Jesse said.

I glanced at him curiously, and he turned to face me with an easy smile.

"You don't like your girlfriend either?" I asked, feeling oddly happy.

He shook his head almost imperceptibly as he continued to grin at me. "No, Tammy's fine," he said. "I was talking about me not liking your boyfriend. I don't care for him."

"Why not?" I asked.

He shrugged. "Why don't you like Tammy?"

I glanced onto the dance floor where she giggled and carried on with her friends. I didn't know what to say to be diplomatic. "Do *you* like her?" I asked.

He grinned. "I must."

I shrugged. "I don't know why I feel like that," I said. "I think we're just really different."

Again, Jesse and I stared at the dance floor, watching everyone else. I wasn't even looking at him and I still got chills just from standing there.

"I'm protective of you," he said. "I guess it's kind of like I am with Jane. I don't think anyone's good enough for you."

I glanced at Jesse and he gestured to the crowd of athletes that had taken over the side of the dance floor. "I'm sure he's a good guy and everything, but I still don't think he's good enough for you."

"Well, I certainly don't think Tammy Gwinn is good enough for you. Not even close. But it doesn't matter, because it's a moot point."

And that's how flustered and overwhelmed I was.

Moot.

I said it in a moment of nervous awkwardness.

I cringed inwardly, smiling at myself.

"What does that even mean?" he asked.

"A moot point. It means there's no point."

"I know what moot point means. What's it got to do with me staying with Tammy?"

I glanced at him, truly trying to think of what I could say in response to that. I was shaken from accidently saying the dreaded word in an actual sentence. I had the thought that everyone in the world knew *Jessie's Girl* was the only song with that lyric, so I was almost convinced I had given myself away by saying the word at all.

"I like Tammy," I said, trying to smooth things over. "She's really pretty. I'm sure she's nice, too."

Just then, as if she heard me, Tammy looked in our direction, first finding Jesse and then leveling him with a wide-eyed smile from across the dance floor. She gestured to him in such a way that said she would be back in a minute. I saw him give her a

41

little wave from the corner of my eye as he stood next to me, but I didn't look at him.

The impromptu photo shoot must have wrapped up, because just after she did that, Barrett turned to find me. He noticed I was standing next to someone, and I watched as his expression shifted from a hint of suspicion to one of relief when he noticed it was just my cousin.

If he only knew.

If he only knew about the utter army of butterflies that had been unleashed in my body as a result of standing next to Jesse.

Barrett smiled and gestured for me to go out there and meet him on the dance floor. He even swayed his shoulders a little, trying to entice me.

This made me do the right thing, which was smile at him and nod that I would be right over. I looked at Jesse. I took a deep breath. I could see my own chest rise and fall even though I hadn't meant to breathe that deeply.

"Guess I'll see you at the shop," he said.

My smile broadened as I nodded. "Yep. I'll be in and out some next week. Mostly back in the office."

"I have an office," Jesse said.

"I know. I saw it when I was there earlier." I reached out to hug him goodbye. "Love you," I said. "You look really handsome." The *love you* part was normal since I had been saying it to him and the rest of my family since I was born, but the *handsome* part was perhaps the most unexpected and goofiest thing I could have said. It happened to be what I was thinking at the moment, so it just popped out.

"Thank you," he said, hugging me back. "And I love you, too." He touched my chin, looking at my face. "I'm not even going to use the word beautiful to compliment you back, though, because it's not good enough, Rose. You're a work of art."

I smiled at him regretfully. I didn't mean to show my disappointment, but I couldn't help it. I could see that he was trying ignore his attraction to me the same way I was trying to ignore my attraction to him—at least I imagined and hoped that's what he was doing.

"See ya soon," I said with extreme reluctance as I started walking toward Barrett.

"Yep, see ya soon," Jesse replied.

And just like that, I turned to walk out onto the dance floor. They were playing an up-tempo song and Barrett swayed his shoulders as he waited for me. He was way on the other end of the dance floor, so it took me a minute to make my way to him.

"What were you doing for so long?" he asked.

"I was talking to Jesse," I said. "And then it was a far walk."

"A far walk?" he asked, smiling and teasing me as I moved my shoulders to the beat. Barrett reached out for me, and I danced with him, letting him turn me around.

We were on the very back edge of the floor, so I got a view of the hallway when he spun me around.

It's funny how the human brain works. I only glanced down that hallway for what must have been two or three seconds max, but I knew what I saw. It was Tammy, and she was with Tyler. I had only seen them for a few seconds, but I saw a flask, and I knew what was going on. I made a mental note not to ride in the truck if Tyler was driving.

I was thinking of everything I had just seen while trying to continue to dance and act normal in front of Barrett. He spun me around again, and I glanced down the hall just long enough to see Tammy reach up to kiss Tyler on the cheek. They both turned to head back toward the dance floor, and I quickly looked away so that she wouldn't catch me watching them.

My heart was pounding.

That strumpet.

I had no idea what to do.

The kiss was more of a flirty, thankful kiss than a passionate one, but they were most certainly getting into trouble back there in the hall, and I felt the undeniable urge to march right over there and call her out on it. I certainly wasn't perfect, but she was nowhere near good enough for Jesse.

Chapter 5

I was thankful for the dim lighting of the dance floor, because my blood pressure was through the roof. I knew I had a red face. The band had changed songs to a ballad, so I put my forehead against Barrett's chest while I regained my composure and thought of what to do.

After a minute, I glanced to the side and saw that Tammy had met up with Jesse. She walked into his arms right when I glanced over there, and I couldn't bear to look. I stared down at the wood floors beneath my feet. I was woozy and short of breath.

"I'm not riding home with Tyler if he's driving," I said.

"He's not. He's getting loaded. He already gave Smitty his keys." He looked down at me. "I was actually going to talk to you about that. I might get a ride home with Kevin and them if that's okay. He's leaving in a minute, and I want to go home and get some rest."

"I think that's smart," I said. "You're gonna have scouts at the game."

"Good. So do you think you and Rebecca could get a ride home with your cousin? I saw he was here. Kevin's only got room for four, and two other guys are already riding with him."

I paused and looked around, feeling totally thrown off by the fact that I apparently had no ride.

Rebecca was on the dance floor, dancing with one of our friends she recognized from school. It sunk in that Barrett had just asked me to get a ride home with Jesse and Tammy, so I turned to look at them. They were looking at each other when I caught sight of them, and I felt desperate to stop him from smiling at her like that.

"Sure," I said. "We'll ride with Jesse." Truth was, I had no idea if we'd be able to ride with him. Plus, there were at least three other people at the reception that I would ask for a ride before I asked Jesse.

Barrett left with his friends.

A whole group of basketball players left at the same time, and I smelled mischief in the air, but I didn't say anything. I talked to Rebecca and told her we were on our own for a ride home. She walked with me to the place where Jesse was standing with Tammy and some of their friends.

Jesse was facing the opposite direction, so he didn't see me approach. Tammy gestured towards me when she saw that I was planning on talking to them, and Jesse turned.

"Hey," I said.

"Hey," he returned, glancing behind me as if expecting to see Barrett.

"He had to leave with one of his friends," I said. "Hey, I see a couple of my other friends, but I was just wondering when you guys were leaving."

"Do you need a ride?" Jesse asked.

"Not if you don't have room or whatever. I see some other people I could ask."

Jesse glanced around as if looking for Barrett again. He was definitely annoyed. "You mean that guy brought you here and left you here without a ride? He drove you here and left without you?"

I shrugged. "We rode here with one of his friends, and I wasn't interested in riding back with him, anyway." I looked directly at Tammy when I said the last part of that sentence, but she just stared at me like she didn't know what I was talking about. "Tyler," I said, still looking at her and feeling brave. "We rode with Tyler."

I remembered the way she drank and flirted with Tyler in the hall, but she just stood there and stared at me like I had lost my mind.

"And they left without you?" Jesse asked, shaking his head as if he just couldn't believe it. His green eyes stood out against his dark suit. He had on his glasses, and they perfectly framed his eyes.

"It's really no big deal," I said, looking away from his gaze before meeting it again. "I just wanted to see what time you guys were leaving."

"You can give them a ride home, but I'm staying here," Tammy said. "You can go do it as long you come back and pick me up."

"You sure?" he asked.

"No, no, no," I said. "I see other people I could ask. I just thought maybe if y'all were leaving."

"I'll take you," Jesse said. "I don't mind."

"He doesn't mind," Tammy said, stretching up to kiss his cheek.

"Just let me know when you're ready," he said to me.

"I'm ready when you are," I said. "Barrett's already gone, and I really don't know either of these people.

"Oh, Kara's so great!" Tammy said, talking about Randall's new wife. "She's the sweetest person you'll ever meet."

I smiled at her. "I'm sure she is."

I did not like her. It was incredibly difficult for me not to spill my guts about what I had seen in the hallway. I resisted the urge to call her out, mostly because I knew she'd deny it.

We walked to the parking lot and got in Jesse's truck. He had a new Chevy. I had seen it but had never ridden in it. There was a bench seat, so I climbed in first, taking the spot next to Jesse while Rebecca sat by the window.

"Do you mind if I play the radio?" I asked.

Jesse didn't bother answering because I didn't wait for him to. I reached out and switched on the radio, which was tuned to a station playing the blues. I wasn't surprised because that's what he'd been raised around.

"Sounds like your mom," I said.

"Jane, too," he said.

I nodded as I settled back into the middle seat. Jesse had changed positions while I was leaning forward to turn on the radio, and I accidently leaned back on his arm. He moved so I could adjust, but he left his arm in a relaxed position that made contact with mine. I made my movements carefully so as not to fully break contact with him.

It was pitiful how utterly affected I was by touching him. It was my arm brushing against his in the front seat of a pickup truck, for crying out loud, and my stomach was tied in a thousand knots because of it. He wasn't touching me intentionally, but he certainly wasn't making the effort to move his arm, either. I sat there as he drove, feeling all sorts of butterflies.

We talked about the wedding and the fact that the whole basketball team showed up at the reception unexpectedly. Jesse asked me more about what I was going to be doing for the family business, and I elaborated on that.

We were about a mile from my apartment when I did something crazy. Sure, I was currently sitting next to him. But at the rate we had been going during the past several years, this was as close as I would get for a while. I knew I would be working at the shop, but I had no idea when I would be in this proximity again. It was for this reason that I justified doing that crazy thing.

It started with me leaning against him to rest my head on his shoulder. The contact seemed very innocent and cousin-like until Jesse reached up and put his hand right on the side of my face, securing it to his shoulder. Maybe he meant that in an innocent way, too, but it caused my heart to beat ever so rapidly.

His hand, warm and big, and soft yet callused, wrapped around my cheek, gently holding me. It caused an ache to happen in my body the likes of which I had never experienced. I was absolutely stricken by Jesse. Totally lovestruck.

As if it were a normal thing to do, I put my hand onto his, holding it in place on my cheek. We rode like that for the next minute or two, staring at the road with our hands intertwined, until we pulled up at my apartment.

I got out of the truck right behind Rebecca. I looked over the seat and told Jesse goodbye, thanks, and that I would see him the following week at the shop. He offered to get out to walk us to the door, but I stopped him since our apartment was clearly visible from the truck, and he could watch us go inside.

Jesse waited until we were inside the apartment with the door closed before he pulled away—I saw his headlights begin to move after we were safe inside.

"What was that?" Rebecca asked.

"What was what?" I asked, taking my shoes off and flexing my aching feet.

"In the truck," she said, taking hers off as well. "With your cousin. Wasn't that your cousin?"

I hesitated, but then smiled and shrugged nonchalantly as I headed toward my bedroom. "Yep," I said. "But not my real cousin. He's so sweet for giving us a ride home."

"Is that Jane's brother?" she asked.

I nodded. "Her twin."

Rebecca had met Jane several times because sometimes I kept Shelby at our apartment rather than Jane's.

"They don't look like twins," she said.

"You don't think so?" I asked absentmindedly.

As we talked, we headed across our small living room to the hallway that led to our bedrooms. Neither of us discussed the fact that we were going to change; we both just assumed we would get out of our dresses and head to our rooms.

"Nope," she said. "I would have never even guessed they were siblings much less twins."

"I think they look alike," I said. "I can see it."

She shrugged. "What's up with him holding your hand like that?" she asked.

"He didn't hold my hand," I said, feeling all sorts of delightful feelings at the fact that we were obvious enough for her to bring it up.

"In the truck," she said. "I glanced over, and you two were holding hands."

"No we weren't," I said.

She shrugged as if to say that she knew I was withholding information, but she was willing to let me off the hook.

"He's really fine," she said. "I wouldn't blame you for flirting with him. I see how he got that Tammy girl to go out with him."

"First of all, he's not my real cousin, and what's that supposed to mean about Tammy?"

"It means I see how he got that supermodel looking girl to go out with him. He's fine. Like Tom Cruise."

"He does not look like Tom Cruise," I said.

"He's as fine as Tom Cruise," she said.

"Yeah, but they don't look alike. And that girl's not a supermodel. I don't even think she's all that."

Rebecca smiled at me and pointed at my chest. "You don't like her," she said.

"You're right, I don't. She doesn't deserve Jesse." My tone was so serious that Rebecca glanced at me with an expression that said she thought I was being a little intense. "I saw her getting wasted with Tyler in the hallway. Then she kissed him right before she went out there with Jesse again."

"She *kissed him*?" Rebecca asked in shock. "You saw your cousin's girlfriend kiss someone else? Why didn't you tell him?"

I let my shoulders slump because I didn't know the answer to that question. "I don't know," I said. "I guess I thought she would just deny it, and it would look like I was just trying to break them up."

"But you kind of are," she assumed, having no idea how accurate she was.

Chapter 6

In addition to my new project with Bishop Motorcycles, I was working and going to school full-time. I was completely exhausted after my first week of research at Bishop. In hindsight, maybe I should have waited until after finals to get started on this personal project, but I had always been impulsive, and once the business venture idea hit me, it was impossible to stop myself from pushing forward with it.

I was actually a bit thankful that Barrett's last game of the season was way out-of-state because I was too tired to go to it if it had been anywhere close by.

It was now Saturday, and I had been in the conference room at Bishop Motorcycles all morning. I had been in and out all week, but I wasn't even close to being done with some goals I had for the week, so I went back on Saturday.

The showroom was open, and there were some employees on the premises, but it was nowhere nearly as busy back in the offices as it was Monday through Friday. It was now three in the afternoon, and I had been in the back all day and had hardly been noticed or interrupted.

Max was one of Uncle Michael's best friends who had been with the business since the very beginning. He loved the company and worked a lot, so it made sense that he would be there on a Saturday. He had come in a couple of hours before and given me half of a sandwich, which was a lifesaver since I didn't think about bringing lunch and was starving.

"Still here?" Max asked peeking his head in later that afternoon.

"Yes sir." I dropped my pencil and stretched, smiling at him.

"You should probably stop staring at paperwork for a little bit." He nudged his head in the direction of the shop. "Come on in there and get your hands dirty. I'm working on an old bike—one of Michael's first models from up in Detroit. You should come help me out."

I smiled. I had grown up around the garage with my dad and had fond memories of assisting—at least I thought of it as assisting. Looking back, I probably did more plundering than actual assisting, but I had happy memories of being in the garage either way.

Max smiled and shrugged. "Betty's got some women over at the house playing bridge this afternoon," he said. "I'll be working on that bike for the next few hours. If you need a change of scenery, come see me."

I looked down at my attire, which could easily be rearranged to apply more to the garage. I smiled at him. "I'd love to, actually," I said. "Barrett's playing in North Carolina tonight, and I don't know how much more of this stuff I can stand." I glanced down at the papers, which were spread out on the table in front of me. "I don't want to start getting careless."

Max patted at the door and shot me a kind smile. "I'll be in there. Just come in whenever you finish up."

I thanked him and almost instantly started wrapping up my work.

I spent the next three hours re-learning the ropes in the garage with Max. He was a patient instructor, who seemed to enjoy teaching me the basics. I had grown up around the garage, but I somehow never really took in what they were doing. I learned more in those three hours with Max than I had in all the previous years I'd been hanging around up there.

I had on jeans and a long sleeve t-shirt when I went in to work that morning, but it was warm in the garage, so I had shed the T-shirt since I had a tank top underneath.

While we were working, I had to get on the ground to reach a part, and when I did, Max threw me a bandana to tie around my head. I made a do-rag out of it, which was still currently in my hair.

I was dirty and greasy, and I had been handling tools and parts and learning a ton for the past few hours. The radio was playing rock-and-roll music, and Max and I were having some good, clean, motorcycle-building fun.

"You're such a natural," Max said.

"You're a great teacher," I said. "Thank you for coming in there to get me. This has been such a welcome change after staring at numbers all week."

"You should see yourself," Max said, grinning as he took a bite of whatever he had just taken out of his lunch box. "You look like Ivy when Michael first started teaching her about motorcycles. She used to get it all over her face like that."

I touched my cheek. "I have it all over my face?" I asked. "What is it? Grease?" I was holding a dirty towel and a crescent wrench, and I tried unsuccessfully to see my face in the silver surface of the wrench.

"The bike's got a mirror attached to it," Max said, smiling when he saw me doing that.

I glanced at him, and he held out the Tupperware container. "Betty sent some food."

I smiled and shook my head before standing to look at myself in the mirror. I was still in motion and was just about to tell Max that I couldn't possibly take his food after he had already fed me lunch, but before I could get the words out of my mouth, I heard a loud police siren.

"Intruder alert! Intruder alert!" Elvis called before making the loud siren noise three more times.

The bird had said a few things to us since we'd been in the garage, but this outburst was loud and sudden, and it startled me. I glanced at Max who was laughing at my reaction and the fact that the bird did that in the first place.

"I know you're in here, Max, I see your truck," Jesse called from the door.

We couldn't see him from where we were, but Elvis's warning was unmistakable, and I knew his voice.

"You better watch out for what I teach him to do when *you* come in..." Jesse trailed off when he came far enough into the room to see me and take in the scene.

Max and I had music playing, and both of us were standing around the old bike, which was partially taken-apart. Jesse had been smiling when he came in and was making the statement about teaching the bird something, but his expression changed to a more serious one as he stopped to regard us. I watched as he walked toward us with a look of growing concern.

"What are y'all doing? Why are y'all in here?"

My heart raced, and I started thinking of all the things I wanted to do right then including check my own appearance in the mirror. All I could do, however, was stand there being speechless.

Max reached over and turned down the music before holding out the plastic container in Jesse's direction. "Want some?" he asked. "Betty made 'em."

Jesse shook his head. "No thanks."

Max held the container out to me, and just because I thought it might push Jesse's buttons, I reached out and took one, popping it into my mouth.

"Thank you," I said. It was some little bite-size piece of finger-food Betty had prepared for her bridge game, and I chewed it with a thankful smile and nod aimed at Max.

"What are y'all doing here?" Jesse asked. He stared at me and then Max, looking somewhat uncomfortable with our presence in the garage.

"I came up here to work on this old bike," Max explained. "It's the one your dad found last week. Rose had been back in the office all day, so she decided to come help me out."

Jesse continued to take everything in, staring at me with a look of caution or confusion, or both. "Since when are you coming here to build bikes?" he asked.

I let out a nervous laugh at his seriousness.

"Seriously, I thought you were in the math department, Rose." He gestured to the hallway that led to the offices. "I thought you we're going to be back there in the office doing math stuff the whole time."

I gave him a challenging, sideways glare. "I quite like working on motorcycles," I said.

"And she's great at it, too," Max said. He reached out and rubbed my head. "A natural."

We'd been having fun and cutting up for the past few hours, and I could see that our situation annoyed Jesse. I didn't know what about it annoyed him, but something did—I could see it in the way the muscles in his jaw flexed, indicating that he was clinching his teeth.

He stared straight at me with those piercing green eyes. "I thought you said you were gonna be in the back doing math," he said.

He seemed totally serious, and I felt vulnerable under his scrutiny. "I was. I am. Max just saw that I'd been back there all day, and he tried to be nice by asking me if I—"

"It's no skin off your back if she helps me out in here," Max said to Jesse.

Jesse turned to walk off, headed toward his own workstation. "Yes, it *is* skin off my back," he said. "She said she was going to be back there doing math. I don't want her in here looking like that."

We still had music playing, and Jesse trailed off as he walked away, but there was no mistaking what he said. I glanced at Max who shrugged as if he hadn't really heard what he said. "Somebody's grumpy," Max mumbled with wide eyes. He held the container in front of me again, and I took a bite of the food despite not being hungry.

I wanted to say something, but I was totally thrown off. My heart was beating like crazy and maybe a little broken, too. "I guess I probably should be going," I said.

Max shook his head. "Don't let Jesse scare you off," he said. "I don't know why he's even acting like that. He's gonna be gone soon, anyway. He usually doesn't come in on Saturday." Max lifted his chin to yell across the room. "What are you doing here, Jesse?"

"I'm meeting Pa," Jesse yelled back without turning around. "Were going fishin'."

Max looked at me with a shrug. "I guess they're going up to the cabin."

I took the bandana off of my head, and shook out my hair, running a hand through it as I leaned down to check myself in the motorcycle's rearview mirror. Max was right. There were black smears on my face. Maybe it just made me look grimy, but I told myself I looked cute that way, and Jesse had been testy because he was overwhelmed with desire. I smiled at myself for wishing such a thing. I wiped at the grease with my fingertips before Max handed me a paper napkin from his lunch box.

Elvis had a better view of the door than we did because he announced that someone was coming in before we could see them. Jesse had only been there for a minute before I heard Elvis start squawking again.

"Glory, hallelujah!" the bird said. "Glory, hallelujah!"

I glanced at Max, who gave me a satisfied smile. "Your grandpa's here," he said, looking real proud of himself.

"Does he say that to everybody who comes in here?" Pa asked as he came into the room.

Out of respect or maybe just because of the fact that Pa didn't have the loudest voice anymore, Max reached over and turned off the radio completely.

"Hey, Mr. Lewis!" Max said. "Nope, he just says that for you and Jacob since y'all are preachers.

This caused my grandfather to smile in amazement as he regarded the bird. Then he looked at us. I could see when he caught sight of me for the first time and surprise sank in.

"Hey there Rose, baby. You're here, too! I thought you might go to that game tonight in North Carolina."

"No sir," I said, walking toward him to give him a hug. "I stayed here to catch up on some work."

"I didn't know y'all would be in here," he said, hugging me.

"I've been really busy with work and school, and then I started doing this project here at Bishop. I've been staring at nothing but numbers all week. I see them when I close my eyes. Mr. Max asked if I wanted to help him take apart this old bike, and I'm really thankful I did."

"Jesse and I are going out to the cabin to do some sunrise fishing in the morning," he said. "We'll be back by tomorrow afternoon if you want to come with us, sweetie. It might be just the thing if you've had a long week."

My grandpa and Jesse had always been close and I knew they went fishing at the cabin on a regular basis. Seeing as how I did my best to limit my exposure to Jesse over the years, I had never gone with them.

"What do you think?" Pa asked Jesse as he walked toward us.

"Think about what?" Jesse asked, having no idea what we were talking about. "Rose working here? I'm good with it as long as it's in the math department." He smiled at me as he came to stand next to us, and I squinted at him, which entertained him even further.

"Math is exactly what she needs a break from," Pa said. "I was talking about her coming fishing with us. What do you think about that?"

Jesse glanced at me. Both of us were taken aback by Pa's suggestion, but we tried not to let it show.

"You mean tonight?" he asked.

"Why not?" Pa asked. "If she wants to. She said she sees math when she closes her eyes. I thought maybe fishing would do her some good—maybe it'd be just the thing."

"I think you're right," Jesse said, smiling at me like he knew I'd never agree to it.

I nodded. "I think you're right, too," I said, calling his bluff.

Pa clapped his hands together. "Great," he said. "So you want to come?"

"I might," I said, nodding.

"It's pretty rustic," Pa warned. "I don't know if you remember it, but it's—"

"They did put in running water," Max interjected, teasing me.

"There's an air-conditioner," Jesse said.

"We did put in a couple of new window units last year," Pa said. "But it's still pretty cool at night this time of year. I don't know that we'll even need them."

"You coming?" Jesse asked.

"What do you think?" Pa asked.

I shrugged. "What do you think?" I asked. I looked directly at Jesse when I said it.

"I think you should come if you want to," he said.

He was so sincere yet nonchalant that I had mixed feelings about it. The bottom line was that I really wanted to go. I loved both of those men and wanted to spend the day with them fishing at the cabin.

I smiled. "Are you sure there's room?"

Chapter 7

"What's going on?" Rebecca asked.

She had been in the bathroom when I came into my apartment in a hurry. I glanced up to see that she was dressed to the nines for her date.

"You look so good," I said.

She smiled. "Thanks. We're going to see that Chevy Chase movie."

"That should be funny," I said, throwing some pajamas into my overnight bag.

"Where are you going?"

"To the cabin," I said. "Pa and Nana have a little cabin. It's out past Dyersburg, about an hour-and-a-half from here. We used to go out there more when I was little. I haven't been in a long time."

"And that's where you're going right now?"

I nodded.

"Who's going?" she asked.

"Just me, Pa, and Jesse, I think. It was gonna be just Pa and Jesse, but they came by the garage on their way out of town, and Pa invited me to go with them."

"What about his girlfriend?" she asked.

She was just doing it in an effort to get a rise out of me, and I squinted at her. "She's at the game," I said. "Same as my boyfriend."

"They should be playing soon," she said.

I nodded. "I'm sure we'll listen to it on the trip as long as we can pick up the station. Pa follows Memphis basketball."

"Are you spending the night up there?" she asked.

"Yep," I said, tossing my duffle bag over my shoulder. I knew the guys were waiting outside, so I had been in a hurry. I sighed as I reached out to give her a hug. "I'm stopping by the bathroom to wipe a washcloth over my sweaty-self and pack my shampoo and stuff. I really could use a shower before we go, but they're waiting downstairs."

"I was just gonna tell you how cute you looked."

I stared down at the lightweight button-down blouse I had just put on in place of my dirty tank top. "Thank you. I've been sweating, but I'm already holding them up. I have to go."

"Go," she said with a smile.

***

"I wanted to get you a chocolate milk shake, but Jesse said you wanted strawberry." Pa said when I got to the truck a few minutes later.

Jesse was driving, and Pa got out so that I could climb into the middle seat. I tossed my bag onto the floorboard before settling in. I peered at the cups, trying to see through the lids so I knew what kind of shake they settled on. It looked like there were two vanillas and a strawberry, and I had no idea which was one was supposed to be for me.

"I like both," I said. "Either would be great."

"But you really wanted strawberry," Jesse said. "Tell him."

"I hope he's right," Pa said, settling in next to me with a groan. "Because that's what we got you."

"Strawberry is my number one favorite," I said. I smiled at my grandpa. "But vanilla is a close second. Chocolate's good too, actually. You can't go wrong with any milkshake, really. I'll even be happy with something weird, like mint or coffee. I've never met a milkshake I didn't like."

I put a straw into the one that looked pink and took a sip out of it. "Thank you," I said.

Jesse had the bag of food in his lap while we were getting on the road, but he handed it to me, and I distributed everyone's burgers. We ate fast food burgers and fries in the front seat of Jesse's truck. We shared the fries, and Jesse was eating without taking his eyes off the road, so at one point, our hands accidently made contact when we were both reaching into the little paper sleeve. We clumsily tried to get out of each other's way.

"Go ahead," I said, holding the fries in front of him. "Actually, no," I said, pulling them away. "Let me..."

I took one of the fries and dipped it into his milkshake. There was a popped-open, vanilla milkshake just sitting there, waiting to be used as a dip, so I dipped it. Jesse thought I was just helping him out so he could drive. He opened his mouth, thinking he was just getting a standard French fry, and he made a face when he realized it wasn't what he was expecting.

"What in the world did I just eat?" he asked, taking his eyes off the road for a split second to look at me as he chewed.

I laughed at his facial expression as it changed from skeptical to curious. "I'll try one more of those," he said.

"You made a face like you didn't like it," I said.

"Because I wasn't expecting that."

I was still smiling as I opened up his milkshake even more and set it where he could easily reach it. "There. All you have to do is dip it in your milkshake," I said.

He glanced at me. "That's all right," he said with a shrug. "Maybe it was a one-time thing." He took a few fries and popped them into his mouth without dipping them in the milkshake, and I regretted not doing it for him.

We drove for another hour after we finished eating. We tuned into the game some (because Pa and Jesse thought I would want to), but mostly we turned the radio off and caught up with each other.

Being a preacher, my granddad was a seasoned communicator, so there was never a lack of conversation. We had talked the whole time, but hadn't yet mentioned Tammy. The very first thing Jesse said when her name got brought up was, "We broke up."

We were almost to the cabin when this happened. I was thankful it was dark out, because it helped hide my reaction. My head whipped around to look at Jesse, but I looked away as quickly as I turned. I didn't want him to think the news had an affect on me. I did my best to play it cool. I wanted to ask him to repeat what he said, but I waited patiently for Pa to do it instead.

"Those things happen," Pa said simply.

"Yep," Jesse agreed.

"Are you still dating that basketball player?" Pa asked despite the fact that we had already talked about Barrett.

"Yes sir," I said, even though I was sorely tempted to deny it.

We drove down back roads on our way to the cabin and completely dropped the subject of boyfriends or breakups. Jesse told a story about a past cabin experience where he brought some of his friends, and one guy dressed up in a bear costume to scare someone else. The guy was so overcome with fear that he threw a small table at the bear. It missed and instead hit a taxidermy deer head that was hanging on the wall. The head then fell onto Jesse who was standing nearby, watching his buddy get scared. The antler cut a gash at the top part of his arm near his shoulder.

"I still have a scar from that," Jesse said, reaching over with his left hand to prod at the back of his right arm. "We stitched it up ourselves with a piece of fishing line because we were all too afraid to take me to the doctor. We had to glue back one of those antlers."

"How old were you when that happened? "I asked.

"High school."

"Stitching yourself with fishing line," Pa said. "I'm sure I don't want to know half of the stuff that's gone on at this cabin."

Jesse pulled into the driveway and parked the truck.

"I'm sure that's the worst of it," I said.

"Oh, yeah, that's the worst of it," Jesse agreed in a way that clearly said he was lying. "Nobody ever jumped into Everett Lake when they couldn't swim and had to be rescued or anything."

"Lord God, thank you for protecting these precious children," Pa said in an impromptu prayer as we climbed out of the truck.

He reached into the back of the truck and retrieved his bag. It was dark out, but the moon was bright, and we could see each other even though the cabin was empty and dark. Jesse came around the back of the truck, carrying his bag and two fishing rods. I was staring at him when he came to stand next to us.

"There are other rods in the shed," he said, assuming that I was worried about the number of fishing poles he was carrying.

I shrugged. "I just assumed you would catch them and let me reel them in."

He smiled as he shifted to walk past me. "Oh, you did?" He glanced at me, and I nodded, which made him smile even more.

The cabin had two bedrooms and a foldout couch in the living room. I had only been out there when there were far too many people crammed inside of it, so this would actually be the first time I got a bed at all. All my memories of the cabin involved sleeping on a pallet on the floor.

I volunteered to sleep on the couch, but Jesse insisted that he wanted to, so I put my things in the back bedroom before heading to the bathroom to take a shower. The accommodations were simple and fairly rustic, but the cabin was clean, and it had a working shower, which at the moment was all I cared about. I was truly dirty after helping Max at the shop and was so looking forward to a shower. I let the guys worry about getting the cabin situated while I went straight to the back. It was still early, so I didn't put on my pajamas, but I did get the grime off of me, which felt amazing.

By the time I came back to the living room, the guys were sitting around with their shoes off, looking cozy. Jesse was sprawled out on the couch, watching the television, and Pa was sitting at the dining table, smiling at me.

"I guess you won't be going night fishing with Jesse," Pa said gesturing to me.

"Why not?" I asked plopping down on the other end of the couch where I could see them both.

"Because you've already had your bath," Pa said. "Your hair's damp. You might catch a cold."

"It's not that cold," I said. "Plus, I could just dry it." I looked at Jesse. "Are you going fishing tonight?"

Jesse nodded. "Are you coming out there with me?"

"No," I said.

He smiled. "Then why did you bother saying you could dry your hair?" he asked.

"Because I'm too stubborn to let Pa tell me I couldn't go," I said with a smile.

They both knew I was kidding, and my grandpa reached out to tousle my hair when he walked by the couch on his way to the bathroom.

"Why aren't you coming?" Jesse asked when I looked at him.

"Because I already had my bath," I said. "My hair is damp."

I looked at him, wishing he'd say something about what a shame it was for me to stay behind, but all he did was smile and shrug at me as if to say I was missing out.

"I'm gonna call Nana and tell her we made a good trip," Pa said from over his shoulder on his way to the bedroom.

I stared at the television. Jesse had it tuned to some random comedy sitcom. "Whatcha watchin'?" I asked.

"There's only like two channels," he said. "If you adjust the bunny ears, just right, you might get TBS. There are a few movies in the cabinet, too."

He tossed me the remote. "I don't care what you watch," he said. "I'm going out on the dock."

"Are you really fishin'?" I asked.

He nodded.

"From the dock, or in the boat?"

"The dock," he said. "I probably won't catch anything. I just like being out there at night."

Chapter 8

I fully intended to go out on the dock with Jesse, but he'd been out there for while, and I couldn't work up the nerve. I think it was because I wanted something to play out that I knew wouldn't. I pictured the whole scene where I wrapped a blanket around my shoulders and sat next to him on the dock. He would catch fish, and we would laugh and talk the night away. I knew it was just a fantasy, though, since boys always wanted you to be quiet when they were trying to fish.

The idea of it was tempting enough, however, that I took a blanket off of the foot of my bed and stashed it by the front door in case I decided to go out there. "Nana said to give you a hug," Pa said when he finally came out of his bedroom.

I had the television on, but I had just been staring blankly at a commercial, so I turned it down, smiling at my granddad in the process.

"I didn't tell my parents I was coming out here," I said when it crossed my mind that I hadn't talked to them. "I guess Nana will tell my dad."

Pa nodded. "I told her you came with us. She'll tell Jacob when she sees him tomorrow at church."

He came to sit beside me on the couch, and I readjusted and glanced at the clock that was hanging on the wall behind him. "What time are y'all going fishing in the morning?" I asked.

"We'll walk out there at about six-fifteen. I like to be out on the water before the sun comes up."

"That way you're not missing church after all," I said.

My granddad knew I was referring to the beauty of creation, and he smiled at me and nodded. "You're right about that. There's something about being in awe of nature that makes you love, even more, the One who made it. He's an artist." He reached over and patted my leg. He was smiling, and this light-hearted talk of God must have made me feel like I had an open door. I didn't plan on bringing it up, but it just sort of came out.

"Do you ever want to do something so bad that you don't think is wrong but other people do?" I asked. "It's just that one minute, I feel guilty about something, but then I tell myself it's just other people who see it as wrong when it's really not."

He looked at me with sweet curiosity. "Do you want to share with me what it is?" he asked. "That might help."

I shook my head. "It's nothing really specific, I guess. It's just feelings and stuff. I mean, sometimes I just feel guilty for my own feelings—and then I go back and forth, thinking the feelings aren't wrong in the first place, so why waste time feeling guilty about them." I sighed. "Never mind. I don't really know what I'm saying."

Pa leaned over and touched my head. "Guilt, sweetheart, is different from conviction. Conviction is useful, whereas guilt—well, guilt's perhaps one of the biggest time-wasters known to man. It comes in a close second to fear."

"What's that mean?" I asked.

He smiled patiently at me. "I'm a sinner, Rose. My whole career, my whole life's work, is centered on the Lord's kingdom, and I am a terrible sinner just like everyone else. I am not even *close* to being free of sin, Rose. I could easily think of all the things I should feel guilty about, feelings, tendencies, hang-ups... I could think of those things and count myself out of the Lord's service. I could easily become immobile, unusable because of my own guilt. I guess I'm just trying to reiterate that guilt and conviction are different, and you just need to ask yourself which one you're experiencing."

I smiled and nudged him with my elbow. "I never knew you sinned before, Pa." I was just messing with him because everyone in Memphis knew Dan Lewis as *the preacher*. "What if it's something that you don't think is a sin or feel convicted about but others may?"

He smiled patiently at me. "Would you like to share with me what it is?" he asked. "I think I could help you."

I shook my head. "No sir. I just meant theoretically."

He shrugged and patted his heart. "Ask God to show you whether it's guilt or conviction," he said. "There's a difference in the two."

I nodded, and took a deep breath, hoping against hope that I hadn't said enough to clue him in on the fact that I was struggling with feelings for Jesse. I felt blood rush to my cheeks as I tried to remember our last few exchanges and wondered if I had said too much.

"I thought you were gonna go out there fishin' with Jesse," Pa said after a few seconds of silence. I had just been wondering if he was onto me about it, so his suggestion made me inwardly suspicious. "Me? Who? Tonight?"

"I just expected y'all both to be out there when I got off the phone."

"I was thinking about going out there," I said, trying to act casual.

Just to prove that I was in no hurry, I sat on the couch with Pa for another ten minutes. We talked about a lot of things that were nowhere near as deep as guilt and conviction. He had a reputation as being a strict person, but I knew him as a grandpa—one who was kind and reasonable.

"I guess I might head out there," I said once I figured a sufficient enough portion of time had passed. I pretended I was doing it reluctantly when, in actuality, I couldn't wait.

I started to get up from the couch, and my granddad asked me if my hair was dry. I combed my fingers through the long, wavy mass of it. It had dried some since I took a shower, but not all the way, so I went into the bathroom and used the blow dryer for a minute just to appease him.

It was one of those tiny, old hairdryers and it smelled funny, but it blew hot air, and I felt better for having taken the opportunity to glance in the mirror before I went out.

I took the blanket with me. I was carrying it in my hand until I stepped outside the door, but it was cool out, so I wrapped it around my shoulders just like in my fantasy. Okay, in my fantasy there would be harp music and a fan blowing my hair when I shrugged into the blanket, and that didn't happen. On the contrary, the whole transition was fairly ungraceful. I dropped the silver flashlight I was holding, and it clanged to the porch floor and rolled to the edge. I had to chase it before picking it up, and I laughed at myself for getting the trip to the dock started with such clumsiness.

I turned on the flashlight and used it to light my path. It took me a minute to get down to the dock, and I smiled at what I saw. I expected Jesse to be sitting up or standing, but he was flat on his back with his hands under his head and legs crossed casually in front of him.

The dock was smaller and shorter than I remembered. It started up on the shore, but it only stuck out over the water about ten or twelve feet, so Jesse took up the whole end of it.

"I thought you'd never come," Jesse said without picking up his head to look at me.

I stepped onto the dock, turning off the flashlight in the process since the light of the moon reflecting on the lake was enough. Jesse scooted a few inches to the side when I came to stand next to him, but remained laying down. I looked out onto the lake, taking in the whole scene. His line was cast and he had secured the rod to a spot on the dock. I could see his line extended out over the lake, and I followed the clear string until I saw the cork resting on top of the water. I glanced down at Jesse with a smile, and he lifted his eyebrows.

"I stared at the water for a while, but the stars..." he trailed off, pointing at the sky.

I glanced up, smiling at the countless clusters of bright stars that filled the night sky. I had planned on just glancing at them and then looking away, but I got stuck staring once I looked up. I gazed at them for a while until focusing again on Jesse who was still sprawled out near my feet. He grinned at me. He had on jeans and a flannel jacket that was open, exposing his T-shirt underneath.

"Why'd you..."

I was about to ask him why he and Tammy broke up. I got the first two words out of my mouth before realizing that was a horrible first thing to say.

"Why'd I what?" he asked.

"Did you catch anything?" I asked, sitting down next to him and pretending that's what I was planning on saying all along.

"A little trout about that big," I glanced at Jesse to see that he was showing the length of about three inches with his fingers.

I smiled. "Are you gonna cook him?"

"Maybe if I was starving," he said.

"Did you let him go free?" I asked. I glanced at him for an answer, and he gave me a nod.

"I'm not really worried about fishing. I'm just laying out here, thinking."

I, in equal parts, both did and did not want to mention Tammy. I was so torn about it that I just sat there for a few seconds not saying anything. I peeled a piece of splintered wood from the deck and threw it into the lake before stretching out next to him. He scooted over to accommodate me and, in the process, made it so that I had plenty of room to lie next to him without making physical contact.

I carefully positioned myself about as close as I could to Jesse without touching him. We were close enough that I could feel the heat of his arm. "Do you remember that one time when we were out here for Easter, and they hid so many eggs that we looked for them all day?" I asked.

"I think they just told us we weren't done looking because they wanted us to stay outside. I think the cabin was too small for all of us."

I laughed at the memory of our families cramming into that cabin when we were little.

"I remember you would tip the boat," Jesse said.

I sat up onto my elbow and turned so that I could stare at him. "I hate that you remember that. That was not on purpose. I did it like three times growing up. I haven't even gotten in a boat since I was like fourteen because I always feel like I'm gonna tip it over."

He regarded me with a curious grin like that was a fact he didn't know. "You can swim, though, can't you?"

"Of course I can," I said, nudging him as I stretched out next to him again. "You've been swimming with me a bunch of times."

"I know, I thought so, but I thought I'd been in boats with you a bunch of times, too. I didn't know you had a thing about them."

"I don't make a big deal about it. I just hadn't been on one in a long time."

"Why'd you come fishing?" he asked.

"Because it sounded like a fun thing to do when Pa asked me. Plus, I really did need to take a break from numbers. Between school and work and now this new thing I've started at your dad's place, I'm looking at numbers for like fifteen hours a day."

"Why are you doing that to yourself?" he asked.

I shrugged. "Because I can, I guess. Physically, I mean. As long as I can work without getting careless or making mistakes, I figure I'll take advantage of the hours in the day."

We sat there for a while, staring at the stars.

"I bet the stars are rearranging themselves into math problems," he said, causing me to laugh.

"Bar charts, actually," I said.

"It's okay," he said. "Sometimes I see bike parts."

"How about right now?" I asked. "What do you see now?"

"Stars," he said. "Whole galaxies and universes. It's really amazing, you know? How little we are in the grand scheme of things."

"I know," I said. "There are so many of them."

"Countless."

"Vast," I added. "Awe inspiring."

"Are you gonna go out on the boat with us in the morning?" Jesse asked.

"I don't know," I said. "I might just stay back. I brought a book. I thought about just coming down here on the dock to read."

"You know you're not gonna flip the boat, right?" Jesse asked.

"You sound more confident of that than I am."

"You won't turn us over, Rose. It's just something silly that stuck in your head from when you were a kid, and we take that bigger boat out now, anyway. I mean, stay back and read your book if you want, but just know you won't tip us over. I won't let you—especially not with granddad in the boat. I'll just hold you on my lap and trap your limbs if you start spazzing out."

I covered my face and laughed at the thought of it. "As tempting as that sounds, I might just stay safe on the shore and read my book."

"What about it sounds tempting?" he asked.

"What?" I asked, stalling.

"What about that scenario sounds tempting to you, Rose?" he repeated.

My heart was beating like crazy. "I was being sarcastic," I said. "…about having to be restrained."

"Oh, okay," he said.

He was so confident and serious, and I had no idea how to respond. I just stared at the stars with my heart beating at least double speed. Several long seconds passed.

"Why'd you break up with your girlfriend?" I asked, finally.

Chapter 9

"You mean Tammy?" Jesse asked. "How do you know I broke up with her?"

"Because you told us."

"I just said we broke up. How do you know she didn't break up with me?"

I sat up, keeping the blanket wrapped around my shoulders as I spun around and landed in a cross-legged position with my knees against Jesse's side.

"Because you were too good for her," I said. "It makes no sense that she would be the one to break up with you."

Jesse readjusted so he could more easily see me. "What about you?" he asked.

"What about me?"

"You're too good for that guy."

"Pa doesn't think so," I said.

I glanced at Jesse, and he smirked at me. "Pa just likes to ask you about your life. And he likes basketball. If anything, he…"

"He what?" I asked.

"Nothing," Jesse said.

I poked his arm. "You can't start to say something, and then say 'nothing'," I said.

He smiled. "I just did."

I squinted at him, and just when I was about to make him tell me what he was about to say, we heard the telltale whizzing, zipping sound of the line as a fish took off with the hook. Jesse sat up and grabbed the rod and reel before I even knew what was going on.

"It's just another little one," he said once he had the chance to fight with it for a few seconds. "Do you want to reel him in?"

I felt comfortable and content wrapped in that blanket, and I really just wanted to sit there and watch Jesse do it, so I shook my head, and he finished the job of catching the fish. It ended up being larger than he originally thought, and as it got closer, he offered it to me again.

We both stood up and got to the edge of the dock as Jesse fought for the catch. It was a nice-looking trout, but Jesse threw it back. Not before he let me pet it, though. I reached out to touch its scaly skin, feeling jumpy like Jesse might threaten to throw it at me. He held it perfectly still so I could touch it.

"Is he gonna be fine?" I asked, staring at the fish.

"Yep," Jesse promised. He gently tossed the fish into the water, stooping to dip his hands in the lake to wash them off.

"He swam away," I said.

Jesse smiled. "That's what they do."

"Unless you eat them," I said.

"We'll probably eat the ones we catch tomorrow," Jesse said. "It makes Pa think he's getting his money worth out of this place when he eats what we catch. Nana usually gets a couple of meals out of it."

"By the time you pay for the cabin and buy gas to come up here, you could have just gone up to the store and picked up about a month's worth of gourmet trout.

Jesse squinted at me and hit his own chest in that funny, male-territorial way. "What are you talkin' bout, girl?" he asked. "We're here to provide for our family."

"No really, I think it's cool that he hangs onto this place. I forgot how much I like it out here. And I'm glad you do this with Pa. I didn't know y'all came out here so often."

Jesse shrugged and absentmindedly put down the rod. "Twice a year just for a night," he said. "Spring and fall. It doesn't seem like a lot, but it rolls around before you know it. I do it with dad, too, and I have a couple of friends who come with me up here. I come up five or six times a year usually."

"Huh, that's crazy. I haven't been in a long time."

"Are you coming with us in the morning?" he asked.

"No. But not because I don't feel welcome."

"Was it because I threatened to restrain you in the boat?" he asked.

"No," I said simply. I stared at him with a completely serious expression that matched his own.

This made him grin a little. "Why then?"

I pointed at the dock below our feet. "Because I like the idea of sitting out here and reading at sunrise. Or maybe I'll sleep in." I shrugged. "Either way, you guys get to have your male bonding, and I get a few hours to do anything but research."

That comment made Jesse ask me something about my job at the bank, which led to other topics like music and food and movies. We went from standing, to sitting, to lying on the dock as we talked and talked and completely lost track of time.

It was midnight when we made our way back to the cabin. Pa was in his room with the door closed and was presumably sleeping. He had pulled out the sofa bed and left blankets and pillows on the couch for Jesse.

"Do you want us to wake you up before we head out?" Jesse asked in whispered tones as we stood in the living room.

I shook my head. "No thanks. I'll set an alarm if I decide to wake up with you guys." I smiled at him and started to walk off toward my bedroom, but he stopped me by reaching out to brush my arm with the back of his hand.

"Rose," he said.

"Yeah?"

He stared at me for several seconds. "Nothing."

I shook my head. "Nothing?" I asked. "You can't do that."

He shrugged. The energy between us was charged with everything we were leaving unsaid.

"What'd you want to tell me?" I asked.

"Just that I had fun," he said as if settling for that. "I'm glad you came with us."

"I'm glad, too," I whispered. I smiled and waved at Jesse as I retreated to my room.

I thought about the conversations I had with Pa and Jesse, replaying different things we said and still not feeling certain how I felt about everything. It took me an hour or so to get settled to the point where I was ready to fall asleep, and even then, it was difficult. The cabin had certain creeks and noises that I wasn't used to, and they made it almost impossible for me to fall asleep.

Finally, I drifted off, only to be abruptly woken up a few short hours later. I was so startled out of my sleep that it took me a second to remember where I was.

I glanced at the clock, which read 3:37, and I blinked, waiting for the noise that had woken me up. I heard commotion, and I got up to see what was going on. I could see as I crossed the living room that Jesse was not on the couch, and the noise was coming from the bedroom where our granddad was staying. I went that way instantly.

I heard a moan before my granddad said, "Ohhhh, push the toes. Push them up, son. Ohhhhh."

I didn't really register that he was talking about toes, and I feared the worst. My heart pounded and I went into panic mode as I tried to figure out what was going on. Jesse was at Pa's bedside and Pa's room was dark enough that I couldn't really see what was happening.

"It's just a cramp," Jesse said, noticing me coming up behind him. Pa made all sorts of noises. First, he made reluctant groans of agony, but then they shifted into thankful sighs.

"Okay, thank you so much, Jesse. I'm so sorry to do that to you, son. I only get those every now and then, but when I do, I need someone else to reach down there and flex my calf for me." He let out another sigh—one that broke my heart hearing it come from my granddad.

"Y'all scared me to death," I said coming to stand next to them with my hand on my chest.

There was a nightlight near his bed, so once I got closer, I could see them perfectly. Jesse sat on the edge of Pa's bed, and Pa laid his head back onto his pillow with another thankful, deep breath. He was not one for drama, and I had never really seen him show any indication of pain, so I stared at him with a concerned expression.

"You sure you're okay?"

"Oh yeah baby, it's just a cramp in my leg. It just hurt until I could get Jesse in here to help me stretch it out. I'm sorry I had to wake y'all up. I just have to have somebody to tilt my toes back."

"Is it feeling better?" I asked.

Pa nodded. "Yes, thank you."

Jesse stood up, looking at me. "We should probably try to get some sleep," he said.

"We certainly should," Pa said, adjusting his covers.

"Are you sure you're okay?" I asked.

"Oh, yeah, Rosie, I'm fine. I'm used to that. It happens to me every once in a while. It's no problem." He paused and glanced at Jesse. "Thank you, Jesse. I'm sorry if I scared you by yelling."

"You didn't," Jesse said with a wave in Pa's direction on our way out.

"Night," I said.

"Night," Pa said.

I stared at Jesse with wide eyes once we turned the corner to head back into the living room. "That freaked me out," I whispered.

He smiled. "Me too, at first, but then I realized what was going on."

I sighed. My heart was still racing. "When I walked in there he sounded like he was in pain, and I don't know, well, since he's an old man I thought that he was...."

"Croakin'?" Jesse asked, teasing me when I trailed off.

His question made me giggle and I leaned back and pushed at his shoulder. "You better get some sleep," I said.

Chapter 10

I tried to get some rest, but I was amped up from seeing Pa in pain. I had been startled from my sleep so I just stayed there, staring at the ceiling and feeling restless.

I was genuinely scared, too, (like the *scared of monsters type of scared*) which rarely happened to me. I kept hearing noises and I had a general feeling of anxiousness. Maybe it was the fact that I had already gotten a few hours sleep before he yelled. Maybe my body thought that's all I needed for the night. Either way, I could *not* fall asleep in spite of lying there and trying my hardest to do so.

I got lost so deeply in my own delirious fears and thoughts that somehow, I convinced myself that it was an okay idea to go into the living room with Jesse. I brought a blanket with me, wrapping it around me the way I had done when we were on the dock earlier. This blanket was bigger, and it was my intention to stretch out on the very edge of Jesse's bed without disturbing him.

I tiptoed into the living room with extreme care. The floors creaked beneath my feet, but it was nothing loud enough to wake him up. He was on his back with his face turned away from me, and I ever so gingerly stretched out on the edge of his bed, trying to barely move it. I was so concerned with being quiet and not causing disturbance that I hadn't been looking at Jesse. I glanced at his face and gasped when I saw that he was staring straight at me with his eyes open.

I made an apologetic expression, which he returned with a reassuring smile.

"You okay?" he whispered.

I nodded. "I couldn't sleep, and I was thinking that since y'all are getting up in an hour, I could just lay out here with you for a little while till I fall asleep."

He took his watch from the end table and focused on reading the time before setting it to the side again. "Why haven't you been sleeping?" he said sleepily as he readjusted to get more comfortable.

"Because I just couldn't," I said.

Jesse pulled me closer to him, encouraging me to rest my body against his, which I did with no hesitation whatsoever. There were, after all, two comforters between us. I snuggled in close to him, feeling completely guilt-free about it.

It was as if I had taken sleeping medicine.

Stretching out next to Jesse caused a warm feeling to envelope me. I was so very comfortable and content with him right there next to me that sleep found me before I even had the chance to go looking for it.

I vaguely recalled hearing Jesse and Pa when they left a little while later. I had already given myself the green-light to sleep in and miss out on the fishing trip, so I was barely even aware when they left.

I woke up at 8:30.

I could have kept on sleeping, but I knew I'd regret it if I didn't get up and enjoy a few minutes on the dock before the boys got back. I made a cup of coffee, and while it was brewing, I tidied up the cabin, folding blankets and putting away the hide-a-bed. (This step was trickier than I anticipated, and I'm pretty sure the bed was a little defective, but I got it done.)

I poured my coffee and added some cream and sugar from little packets that were stashed next to the coffee pot. I took my mug, along with a book and a blanket, when I went out to the dock. It was a beautiful spring morning—one that would was perfect for getting lost in a book.

I sat out there and read for about an hour, and I thoroughly enjoyed the story I was reading, but it was frustrating because I had to constantly stop and reread paragraphs on account of my thoughts wandering back to Jesse.

This exposure to him was just too much. I was in the middle of contemplating ways I could avoid him at the shop when I saw them approaching in the distance—at least I thought it was them. I squinted into the sun, watching as a boat came closer.

They parked the boat on the neighbor's dock, which was much nicer and longer than the one I was sitting on. I turned toward them, waving. Jesse waved back when he saw me, and so did Pa.

Jesse gestured with his finger in the air, and I took it to mean that he wanted me to stay where I was, so I gave him a thumb's up and I sat up, putting a bookmark into my book.

It took Jesse and Pa a minute or two to square away things with the boat, and I watched as they finished up by setting their gear near the truck. They talked for a few seconds before Jesse took off, jogging toward me with a smile. He was wearing jeans and that same flannel jacket with a T-shirt underneath. He strode toward me, smiling confidently and taking my breath away. He was wearing sunglasses, which only added to the picturesque quality of it all.

"How'd y'all do?" I asked.

"We kept about eight," he said. "It should feed the family for a little while."

I laughed at him as he sat beside me on the dock.

"How'd you sleep?" he asked.

"Good," I said. "Once I came in there with you, I slept great." I glanced at him, and he smiled. The way his mouth moved and shifted when he smiled— the way it flashed his gorgeous teeth. I had to look away, and when I did, he reached out to touch my leg. It was just two of his fingers on my knee, but it sent waves of anticipation through me.

"Rose."

I had glanced away, and he said it to get me to look at him again.

I looked at him. I could see his eyes through his sunglasses, and I knew he could see mine, because we stared right at each other.

"I slept good, too," he said.

I smiled and shook my head at him. "Good," I said since I had no idea what he was getting at.

"I slept better after you came in there," he added.

It was exactly what I wanted him to say, and my heart reacted accordingly, feeling like it wanted to leap out of my chest. I looked at him, and he gave me a regretful smile as he shook his head.

"I know you have a boyfriend, Rose, so I'm not trying to—"

"Jesse, it wouldn't matter, anyway."

He scowled when I said that, but he didn't say anything.

I wanted him to insist that it *would matter*. I regretted cutting him off. I wished I had just let him continue with what he was saying.

He breathed a sigh. "It's just that when you were next to me this morning... I just felt like... I don't know what I felt. I felt right, I guess."

"Jesse we're cousins," I said.

"No we're not," he said, grimacing at me. "We're not even distant cousins. We're not even related at all."

He was so matter-of-fact about it that I experienced an instant feeling of elation, which was quickly dampened by the thought we were likely the only two in the whole universe who felt this way about our situation.

I glanced at the cabin and then at Jesse, turning my shoulders a little to face him more fully.

"But it doesn't matter because you have a boyfriend," he said.

"I do, Jesse, but even if I didn't, we couldn't."

"Yes, we can. That's the beauty of it. The other day I was looking at you, thinking about everything, and you know what Rose? I'm *glad* you're not my real cousin."

We made eye contact for the next few seconds.

It was on the tip of my tongue to tell him that I would break up with Barrett in a heartbeat if I thought he meant what he was saying right now, but before I could get the words out, I heard a loud whistle coming from the cabin.

The whistle repeated two more times, and Jesse shot me a worried expression before standing up to head to the cabin.

"I'm gonna go see what he needs," he said, beginning to jog.

"I'm right behind you," I said.

I was already a little on edge from the cramp incident the night before, so Pa's whistle had me worried. I gathered my things quickly and was only a short distance behind Jesse as we headed up to the cabin.

"It's okay, I'm okay!" Pa yelled when he saw that we were headed toward him in a hurry. "It's a phone call that came in for Rose!"

It took a few more seconds for us to get into the cabin, and I was breathless by the time we did.

"What is it?" I asked.

Pa had been looking at me the whole time, gesturing for me to come inside.

"You have a message from your friend," he said. "It's about Barrett, I believe. I just listened to the beginning of it before I went out there and whistled for you."

There was an answering machine lying on the bar, and Pa pressed the button to make the message play. He watched me as he waited for the machine to start. There was a beep and then I heard the sound of my roommate's voice.

"Hi, this is Rebecca, Rose Lewis's roommate. I'm calling to leave a message for Rose. Rose, I don't know if you've heard, but I saw on the news this morning that there's been an accident with some the UM basketball players. I think Barrett was with them. They said his name with the ones who had been involved. Anyway, I think it happened early this morning. I think it was pretty serious, Rose. You might want to look into it and see about getting back when you can. I hope this is the Lewis family's cabin. I had to go up to the church to get the number. I hope I'm calling the right place. This message is for Rose Lewis. This is Rebecca. Thank you."

There was another beep, and I stared at Jesse with a disbelieving expression.

My heart sank. "What do you think happened?"

Pa turned on the TV to see if he could find a news station reporting on it, but there was nothing. I called my apartment, and Rebecca picked up the phone on the first ring.

"It's Rose," I said when I heard her answer.

"Where are you?"

"I'm still up by Dyersburg. What happened?"

"I don't know exactly," she said. "I saw it like an hour ago on the news, and I had to track down the number to call you, so I'm just getting back home. Apparently, there was an accident early this morning. All I know is that multiple members of the basketball team were involved, and I think there were some casualties."

"Casualties?" I asked, feeling like I couldn't have heard her correctly. I couldn't breathe. "You mean somebody *died*?"

"Yes," she said. "I told you it was serious. I don't think it was Barrett. I think he's okay, but you need to call the hospital."

"Were they in the bus?" I asked. "What hospital?" I felt like I was about to lose it, and then my grandfather put a comforting hand on my back.

"I don't know," she said. "I wish I had more information, but I don't. The news reporter was kind of vague. I think they were on their way back to Memphis from North Carolina, but I'm not sure how close they were. I don't think they were on the bus. Maybe you can call Barrett's mom or the police department."

I had no idea what to do or say next so I just thanked Rebecca for calling me and hung up the phone. I looked at my grandfather, feeling like I was in some kind of nightmare.

"She said there's been an accident," I said numbly.

Pa nodded. "We better head back to Memphis."

Chapter 11

I called Barrett's mom before we left the cabin. His family lived in Arkansas, and I didn't know her number by heart, but I had it written down in my purse, so I called her while Jesse and Pa busied themselves, making sure we were ready to go.

I shook as I pushed the buttons to dial the number.

"Hello," a man's voice said.

"Hello, this is Rose, Barrett's girlfriend," I said. I couldn't help but feel a little awkward when I said that phrase in front of Jesse, but my concern about the accident overruled my awkwardness.

"Is Ms. Hall available?"

"She's already left for Tennessee, sweetie," the man said.

I had no idea who the gentleman was. Barrett's mom was a single woman who lived with her sister and I hadn't expected a man to pick up.

I cleared my throat. "I'm sorry, but I've been out of town, and I, uh… was there an accident?"

"Oh yeah, baby, there was," the gentleman said sadly. "It was bad—a bad one. But we heard Barrett's stable, thank the Lord. His mama's already talked to the doctors. They've got him in surgery and should be done by the time she gets there. I think it's his leg. No internal damage. That's what Sheila was saying."

"Is everyone stable?" I asked.

I couldn't get the idea of there being casualties out of my head, and I needed to know.

"Are you talking about the others in the accident?" he asked.

"Yes, you said Barrett was stable. Is that true for everyone?"

I cringed as I waited for him to answer.

"Oh no baby. It was a real bad accident. Two of the boys passed away for sure, and I think one is in critical condition."

"Where are they?" I asked. "Where's Barrett?"

"Memphis. At Methodist Hospital."

I was so overwhelmed that I didn't even ask him who had passed away or for any of the other details. I just thanked him and hung up the phone so I could get in the truck.

We we're collectively silent on the way back to Memphis. Pa talked for a minute about how fleeting this life was, but Jesse and I weren't really responsive, so he dropped the subject pretty quickly. Jesse and I both had our own things going on, so we opted for silence. He turned on the radio and we just listened to music.

We were about twenty minutes from Memphis when we heard the news of the accident on the radio. They said the two names of the guys who had been killed in the accident, and I honestly felt like I was going to throw up when it hit me that these guys actually died. Tyler and Vince. They were two of Barrett's best friends, and honestly, my body didn't know how to respond to the news. I felt nauseous and anxious, like the whole world had turned on it's axis and suddenly I, too, was in danger. I glanced at the speedometer to see how fast Jesse was going just to make sure we weren't about to crash.

The rest of the trip went by in a complete blur.

I cried some and Pa said some comforting things, and before I knew it, we were pulling up at Methodist Hospital.

Jesse hadn't said a word the whole time. I shouldn't have cared enough to notice that, but I did. In the midst of everything that was going on, I still cared about Jesse and wondered how he felt.

Pa got out to let me climb out of the passenger's side, but I stopped and looked at Jesse first. He gave me a little noncommittal smile that said he expected me to smile back before I left.

"I'm sorry we didn't get to finish our conversation," I said.

He gave me another courtesy smile. "It's okay," he said.

Maybe I wanted him to be more disappointed than he was because I hesitated for a second or two even though Pa was waiting for me to get out of the truck.

"I don't know what's waiting for me in there," I said.

"It's fine," he said, glancing out the window at the hospital entrance. "Go do what you need to do."

"I'm sorry," I whispered.

Jesse looked at me. His expression was completely unreadable. I wished I knew what he was thinking. I hopped out of the truck and regretfully waved at him. He gave me a little two-fingered salute, and I turned to find that Pa was standing there with his arms out, waiting for a hug. "I'm sure your parents heard about it, but I'll call and fill them in," Pa said.

I thanked them and hugged Pa before heading inside to see what craziness awaited me.

During the next three hours I stayed with Barrett's mom in the waiting room. I spoke to my parents and got a more detailed account of what had happened in the accident. Apparently, there was bus trouble, so the team could either wait for them to straighten that out or get their own ride home. There were six guys in a rental vehicle when it went off the road and crashed into a tree before flipping several times. Two guys had passed away, two were in critical condition, and two had minor injuries. A guy named Vince was behind the wheel. He and Tyler had been in the front seat.

It was a huge deal with the whole town, and there were crowds of people outside the hospital, lighting candles, holding signs, and bringing flowers. There was already talk of memorial services, and my head was spinning with feelings and details before I even got to see Barrett.

You can imagine how I felt when I got to his room and saw him with his face in his hands like he was crying. He was usually a big, tough athlete who didn't care much for crying.

I glanced at the nurse who had been the one to come get me and lead me to the room.

"He's okay," she said. "He just talked to his mom. He wanted you come in." She smiled regretfully at me and whispered, "He's still coming off of the anesthesia, and he's just learning about the other guys."

I shook my head at her. "I'm not ready for this," I said, pushing a little towards the door since I knew Barrett hadn't seen me yet.

She pushed me in the other direction, toward Barrett. "He's okay," she said. "He needs you right now. He was asking for you."

I went to Barrett's bedside, propping myself on the very edge of his bed. I sat on his left side because his right leg was in a huge, intimidating contraption. He noticed me there, and he leaned toward me wearing a miserable expression that broke my heart.

"I'm so sorry," I whispered, hugging him as he leaned even further in my direction.

"I'm glad you're here," he said.

***

And that was the story of my life for the next two months.

Barrett needed me, and I was there for him.

His mother didn't have room for him in her current situation in Arkansas, and she couldn't take time off work to move to Memphis, so I took care of him.

I reluctantly put off the project at Bishop Motorcycles because it was just too much. It was the end of the semester, and I had to keep up with my schoolwork and my job. It was all I could do just to maintain those and take care of Barrett.

The first few weeks were incredibly difficult.

Barrett was in a lot of pain both physically and emotionally, and for the first week or two, needed to be waited on hand and foot and counseled nonstop.

One of the other guys that was involved in the accident survived at the hospital for little while, but he passed away after the first week. It seemed like I went to one memorial service after another. The town was beside themselves, and so was Barrett.

I was exhausted and disappointed that I wasn't able to finish the project I had started with my uncle's company, but sometimes life just doesn't work out the way you think it's going to. I knew I could get back to it once I finished the semester and things had settled down with Barrett.

It had been two months since the accident, and honestly, I didn't know when that time would come.

I was finished with school and was off for the summer, but somehow my schedule felt just as busy.

Barrett seemed to need my help on a constant basis. His physical therapist said he may never have full function in his knee, and he grew depressed, assuming his NBA career was over before it even began.

I tried to encourage him and stay positive, but it was exhausting. We did not behave like a couple at all, and yet I really didn't feel like there was anything I could do to get myself out of this situation.

I still remembered that conversation I started with Jesse. It was tucked away in the back of my mind, and I wanted more than anything to call him up and continue it, but it had been so long that I wasn't even sure if he wanted to. Seeing as how it was now two months later (and I hadn't contacted him, nor had he contacted me) I was relatively sure our big moment had passed. I hated that, but I tried to keep my chin up.

I had just recently decided that since I was finished with school and Barrett was back on his feet, I needed to get back to the Bishop project. I hadn't told Barrett I was planning on starting up on it again, but he was gaining more independence physically, so I figured it was good timing.

I called Uncle Michael that Friday to see if I could go by the shop and pick up some of the paperwork I had been looking at before the accident.

He was in the garage working on a bike when I called, and he told me to come on by.

I had to go in through the garage because the offices were locked by the time I got there. Uncle Michael was still working, and he unlocked the door and told me to make myself at home in the office. I thanked him and said I would check in with him again on the way out.

I ended up staying in the office for a couple of hours, and by the time I got back, Aunt Ivy was there with him. She was sitting in a chair, watching Uncle Michael work. It was a beautiful evening, and they had two of the garage doors open. They had music playing and were just hanging out while Michael worked.

"Do y'all just come up here and work on motorcycles for fun?" I asked, smiling and thinking about how sweet they were.

"Yes we do," Aunt Ivy said, motioning for me to come sit next to her. "This one's special, though."

"It's for Jane," Michael said.

"She's been wanting this bike for a long time. It's the one with the broken spoke. Her daddy's been working on it for a while. She's coming by to get it tonight."

"Broken spoke," I said. "Wasn't that the name of one of your songs?"

Ivy nodded and gestured to the motorcycle. "I got the name from this bike. That's what the song's about. Jane's always liked it, and it was just sitting over there, collecting dust."

"That's exciting!" I said. "Does she know she's getting it or is it going to be a surprise?"

"Oh, she knows, she's been asking him every day, *when's it gonna be done?*"

"And she's getting it tonight?" I asked.

Aunt Ivy nodded. "She's on her way up here." She looked at Michael. "One of us is going to have to help her get her car home, and Shelby."

Uncle Michael nodded as if he'd already thought of that and said something about knowing where Jane was going for a ride.

As they were having this conversation, I heard the sound of an engine drawing closer and closer until eventually, someone came through the open garage door on a roaring motorcycle and parked it right in our midst.

It was so unexpected that I stared at the person that was driving it, looking at him from the chest down, and not even realizing at first that it was Jesse. He cut the engine and got off the bike, regarding us with a casual smile that didn't reflect any of the anxiousness I felt.

I hadn't seen him in so long that I was breathless and speechless—numb, really. I honestly felt like I couldn't think straight or get a good breath of air into my lungs. Jesse.

Memories of our conversation on the dock came crashing into my mind when I saw his smile. I remembered feeling like he was in my grasp, and I hated the accident and the fact that it derailed everything.

Chapter 12

"Where's Jane?" was the first thing Jesse said as he took off his helmet. He looked around as he finished getting off of his motorcycle, running his hand through his hair as if to make sure the helmet hadn't left it in disarray. Judging from the way my heart pounded, the last two months had done nothing to quench my desire for him.

The sound of Elvis mimicking a siren and then saying, "Intruder alert!" served as a distraction, and I glanced at the bird with a smile.

"Jane's on her way," Ivy said once Elvis stopped squawking. "She stopped to pick up the food."

Something about the way she said it made me realize this was a planned, family get-together. I got up from my stool, picking up my bag with every intention of leaving right then.

"I'm gonna go on home," I said.

"Nooo!" Aunt Ivy insisted. "Jane would want you to stick around. She's picking up food from Van's on her way over here, and we're gonna have plenty. You should stay."

"Ohh, I can't," I said. "I have to be going."

"Your dad said you've been busy helping your boyfriend," Aunt Ivy said, assuming that's where I had to go.

I smiled even though I felt nauseous.

I didn't even look at Jesse.

"Yes ma'am," I said. "He's getting better now, though."

"That's why she's up here working again," Uncle Michael said, gesturing to my bag.

"When'd you start working here again?" Jesse asked.

I looked at him, noticing the unemotional way he leaned against the countertop and regarded me. "I just dropped by to look at my notes from before," I said, glancing around at everyone and feeling shy even though they were my family. I smiled at Jesse. "Today was my first time back," I said, shrugging and patting my bag to indicate that it contained some of my paperwork. I regarded Michael. "I'll look at this stuff over the weekend, but I'm sure I'll be in a little next week, if that's okay."

He smiled and gave me a sweet nod.

"You sure you can't stay?" Aunt Ivy asked. "Jane's gonna be upset about missing you."

I shook my head regretfully. "I just saw her last night, though."

"Oh, that's right," Ivy said. "She said you watched Shelby while she went to band practice."

Just then, we saw headlights shining into the garage through the open door. Jane pulled right into the shop, leaving the back half of her car sticking out. She beeped her horn, which everybody but me had been expecting. Ivy faked surprise by sticking her fingers in her ears and a making silly expression, and Shelby got out of car, giggling at our reactions.

"You almost scared me to death on that one," Ivy said to Shelby, who continued giggling as she ran across the garage, headed toward us.

To Shelby, Aunt Ivy was *Shug* and Uncle Michael was *Doozy*, and she ran up to them, calling their names.

Ivy scooped Shelby up and positioned her on her hip, but my attention was drawn to Jane who was now out of the car. She walked toward us with her hands full of paper bags from Van's Diner. Jesse and I both had the same idea, and we went over there to offer her help. Jane handed Jesse the bags and kissed him on the cheek before reaching out to hug me.

I squeezed her tightly and was about to say something about the fact that I was on my way out, but she turned right around and started walking toward her family, pulling me with her.

"Can you believe this is mine now?" she asked in an awestruck tone.

"No," I said, looking at the beautiful motorcycle. "It's so nice. And I didn't know there was a whole story behind it."

"Oh, yeah," she said, pointing at the wheel. "Dad popped off one of the spokes to make a ring for mom."

We all glanced at the tires even though there was no way we could notice the missing spoke at a glance.

"What was up with Barrett last night?" Jane asked. She scowled as she said it, and then she

111

pulled back so she could look directly at me, waiting for me to answer.

I just shrugged shyly, knowing that everyone was listening to us. "He's just like that," I said. "The draft is coming up, and he knows it's not going to happen for him this year. Not with his leg like it is." I paused and shook my head thinking of all the stuff he had said over the past couple of months. "I don't think he believes he'll play again," I said.

"So that's just how he acts now?" Jane asked still looking at me like she was a bit confused. "Rude?"

I smiled and nodded, trying to remember what Barrett had even said to her the night before. I couldn't recall what he said. "What'd he say to you?" I asked.

She looked at me like she couldn't believe I didn't know. "It wasn't what he said to *me*. It was what he said to you. Do you not remember him getting onto you for forgetting to take back that movie?"

"Oh yeah, but I did it on my way home last night," I said. "It didn't even get a late fee; I don't know what he was so upset about."

Jane still stared at me with a confused expression. "I can't believe he just acts like that."

"He's been through a lot lately," I said, trying my best to delicately get out of the conversation.

I was already mortified by the fact that we were having this conversation in front of Jesse. He was standing right there, listening to everything we said.

I felt like I needed to take up for Barrett, while at the same time I wanted to breakdown and tell them what a horrible person he was.

Shelby giggled as Ivy placed her on the motorcycle, and they all started joking about Shelby being a mini version of Jane. Jane had her arm around my shoulder, but she let go of me to go interact with her little girl.

I felt like it was as good a time as any for me to say goodbye, so I took a step back and prepared to announce my departure. I breathed in to say something, but I saw Jesse step next to me out of the corner of my eye. He stood close enough that I glanced his way instead of making my planned exit. I expected Jesse to smile at me when I did, but his expression remained serious as he glanced at me.

"I'm not okay with him treating you bad, Rose."

I hadn't expected him to say that, so I took a step back shaking my head like it had all been a big misunderstanding.

"Barrett? He's fine, it's fine, I'm just helping him while he gets back on his..."

I trailed off. I tilted my head, giving Jesse a regretful grin.

"What?" he asked.

"I guess its obligation at this point, if you want to know the truth. I'm with him out of obligation. But, hey, people have worse lots in life."

"Oh, so you're just sentenced to be with this guy for the rest of your life?" Jesse asked.

113

His tone was so matter-of-fact that I squinted at him. "No, I'm not. But I also don't know how to talk to him. He's so dependent on me. I don't even want to think about how he'd react."

It was a serious and sincere statement and I had been looking at Jesse with all earnestness when I said it, but I turned with a huge smile when I saw that Shelby was walking towards us. She put up her hands, and Jesse scooped her into his arms.

"Hey Belshe," Jesse said, teasing Shelby by mixing up her name.

She slapped her hand to her forehead. "Shelby!" she giggled.

"I mean Shelby!" Jesse said, correcting himself.

"Hi," she said, squeezing his neck.

I reached out and scratched her little back. "Hi and bye, punkin'," I said.

"Hi Aunt Wose," she said, turning to face me while still in Jesse's arms.

(She called me Aunt Rose even though I wasn't technically her aunt.)

"Hey peanut."

Shelby leaned over to kiss me and I lunged toward her so that I wouldn't leave her hanging. Instead of kissing me like I thought she would, she grabbed a hold of my head, positioning my face right next to Jesse's. She patted our cheeks and smiled contentedly as if she enjoyed seeing us lined up like this. I kissed Jesse on the cheek before leaning forward to do the same to Shelby.

"I love my family," I said, after making the smooching sound on Shelby's cheek. "I'm glad I got to see your new toy, Jane," I announced, waving in the direction of the other three who were huddled around the motorcycle.

"Thank you!" Jane called, waving at me while wearing a disappointed look on her face. "Are you sure you have to go? We have plenty of food, and I can take you for a ride on it if you want."

"She is not ready for that," Michael said, shaking his head and closing his eyes. "Give her a few months to practice, and she'll take you for a ride."

"I'll take you for ride," Jesse said.

He spoke to me and not the others, but Shelby also heard, and she threw up her arms and squealed with delight. "I wanna go!"

Jesse looked at Shelby. "I'll take you around the parking lot in a minute, squirt," he said before focusing on me. "It's too bad you're in such a big hurry. I was gonna take Jane out around Birk's farm. I wish you could come with us."

"You mean on motorcycles?" I asked.

Jesse smiled at me as if we both knew the answer to that question.

"I'm serious," I said. "Are you taking her over there on motorcycles?"

He nodded. "You'd be riding with me."

"Is Rose coming with us?" Jane asked from across the way.

"Yep," Jesse said without even waiting for my answer.

I wrinkled my nose at him, and he gave me a challenging smile.

"What? You know you want to," he said, grinning irresistibly.

"*I want to!*" said Shelby with delight.

"You need to come eat first while your food is still warm," Jane said, digging in the bags.

I glanced at Jesse and gave him a resigned smile before looking at Uncle Michael. "Do you mind if I use the phone in the conference room real fast?"

He was in the middle of helping Jane distribute burgers but he gave me a smile and waved at me as if to say I knew I could make myself at home there.

"Is it locked?" I asked as I went toward the door.

"The office door locked behind you, but there's a phone in the waiting room," Ivy said.

The waiting room was really close to the garage, so I made it there quickly. I ducked inside and took a seat on the row of padded chairs that lined the wall. There was a simple desk phone on a nearby table, and I picked up the receiver and dialed Barrett's number.

He answered on the second ring. "Hello?"

"Hey," I said.

"Where are you?"

"I'm still at my uncle's shop."

116

"I still haven't eaten dinner. I called your apartment, and Rebecca had no idea where you were."

"I told you where I was. I told you I was coming up here to get started on this paperwork."

"I know, but that was like three hours ago."

"That's how long it took me. And I have a lot more to do. I'm going to be up here a lot of hours workin' on this project. I told you that."

"Well, I tried to call the number you gave me, and nobody picked up."

He sounded agitated, and honestly, I was so frustrated that I didn't care. I sighed and buried my face in my hand as I sat there in the mostly dark waiting room.

"I'm sorry nobody picked up, Barrett. I was working. I just finished, and I am calling to let you know that I'm going to eat a bite of dinner with my family and maybe go for a drive."

"A drive?" he asked the question like he must have heard me wrong. "Did you say you're going on a drive?"

"Probably. After we eat."

"I'm really glad you're thinking about me, Rose that's really nice of you. I'm just sitting over here starving and having no idea what you're doing."

"If you're starving, Barrett, you need to stand up, walk out the door, and go get yourself some food. If you can't make it that far, you can just look in your fridge. I put a bunch of food in your fridge." I really wanted to stay and hang out with my family, so my tone was unsympathetic.

He paused for what felt like a full minute before speaking again. "I need you," he said. "I was just getting used to you being home for the summer, and now you're trying to commit to helping your family. You spread yourself too thin."

"I'm not spread too thin," I said. "And I'm not helping them. They're helping me."

"What time are you coming over here?" he asked pitifully.

"A little later," I said. "I was thinking about not stopping by tonight at all. I still have a lot to do with this paperwork."

"Rose, please," he said.

I turned to find Jane standing in the doorway. She was leaning against the doorframe with a cautious expression, and I held my finger up telling her I would just be a minute.

"I can't believe going for a drive is more important to you than helping me out."

"Well, I'm sorry. I'm sad you're giving me a hard time about it."

I looked at Jane with a regretful smile. I was embarrassed to have this conversation in front of her, but at the same time I was happy she came back there. She furrowed her eyebrows when I made the statement about Barrett giving me a hard time, but shook my head as reassurance that I was fine.

"Barrett, I'm going to hang out with my family for little bit," I said. "Jane's right here waiting for me. I'll call you in a little while."

"Okay," Barrett said, knowing my tone was impassive. "But please come by tonight," he said. "I wanted you to take me by Mikey's."

"I don't know what time I'm going to be done," I said. "Maybe you should tell Mikey to come get you."

"Maybe you should try to help me out sometimes," he said, sounding annoyed.

"I do that *all the time*," I said, trying to keep my one-sided conversation vague for Jane's sake.

"Except for when I need some Taco Bell or a ride to Mikey's," he said. He was trying to make it seem like he was joking, but I knew he was being serious.

"Okay," I said. "So I'll call you later."

"Love you," he said.

And, in spite of it perhaps being the most awkward thing that had ever come out of my mouth, I repeated the dreaded, untruthful phrase just for the sake of getting off the phone.

"Love you too," I said, trying to sound like I meant it. I was so disgusted with myself and I hung up the phone without even hearing if he responded.

Chapter 13

I stared at Jane with a completely discouraged look on my face after I hung up. "I'm sorry you had to hear me say that just now," I said.

"Say what? That you love him, or all of it?"

"All of it," I said. "And that I love him. That was a lie. I don't love him. We don't even act like we're in a relationship. He just treats me like his assistant."

Jane sat down on the seat next to me, looking at me with care and concern. "Then why are you dating him?"

"I don't even know."

I closed my eyes and shook my head.

I felt discouraged and exhausted.

It was difficult being stuck in a relationship. It was difficult to constantly help someone who wasn't at all thankful.

"I was seriously about to break up with him before the accident," I said, letting out a sigh. "I was about to do it, and now if I…" I hesitated. "If I did it now, it would seem like I only wanted him when I thought he was gonna get drafted or whatever."

"That's not true. What makes you say that?" she asked.

"Because he's said it," I said. "He was talking about his friend who was in the accident with him, saying how heartless it would be for his girlfriend to leave him now."

Jane made an expression of distaste. "Are you saying Barrett used another couple as an example to make you feel guilty about leaving him?"

"I guess. I mean, I don't know if he meant it that way. I just know I'm not happy. It's been a really difficult couple of months."

"What do your parents say? Did you tell your mom?"

I nodded. "You know my parents. Of course, they say I should pray about it. But I don't really know how God could answer this prayer other than to compel Barrett to break up with me, and I just don't see that happening." I gave her a little sorrowful grin. "I'm really am sorry for unloading on you," I said. "I know we should get back out there. Shelby's gonna be looking for you."

Jane stood up, pulling me up with her. "Don't be sorry," she said as we began making our way back toward the shop. "I want you to tell me what's going on with you. I knew you had been really busy lately, but I didn't know about everything that was going on with you and Barrett. I didn't know how he was acting."

"It's fine," I said as I shrugged a shoulder. "I mean, ultimately it's my choice to be with him."

"That's exactly what I was thinking when you mentioned praying about it," she said. "Obviously, it's good to pray about everything, but sometimes we have to take action, you know? Sometimes we actually have to *do something* about the thing we're praying about. You have to be involved."

We stopped at the door that led to the garage, and she looked at me, waiting to hear how I'd respond.

"Would you think I was a terrible person if I broke up with Barrett at a time like this, after an accident, and just when his dreams got shattered?"

"No, Rose, I wouldn't think that. Because I know you, and I know you're *not* a terrible person. I saw Barrett last night. I saw how he talked to you. I wondered why you were putting up with that."

"He's been through a lot," I said.

"So have a lot of people," she said. "So have I. I married Seth the day before he got deployed, thinking we were doing some big romantic gesture. We were together once, Rose, and he left me with Shelby and went over to Kuwait and got himself killed. I had sex one time, and now I'm a mom and a widow. Things happen to people. Things we don't always understand. It's up to us how we respond to them. That's our choice. Barrett has no right to be rude to you after how much you've helped him out."

She opened the metal door right after she said that, and we walked in, still looking at each other.

"Is everything okay?" Aunt Ivy asked.

I shot her a smile. "Yes ma'am," I said.

"Was it Barrett?" Aunt Ivy asked.

It didn't surprise me that she was so direct about it because we were just that type of family. She had no idea the question would be as awkward as it was because she had no clue about my feelings for Jesse.

Neither did Jane for that matter, which was why the next thing out of her mouth was, "She's about to break up with him, anyway."

Everyone looked at me as if waiting to see if I would confirm Jane's statement. I felt myself blushing.

"I wish I could," I said honestly.

Jane shook her head as she took a bite of burger and then chewed a big mouthful. "I saw firsthand what a little stinker he was being. She needs to just go ahead and cut her losses. She's just got to find the right way to do it."

"Who was being a stinkew?" Shelby asked.

"Aunt Rose's boyfriend," Jane said.

I wasn't very fond of this conversation, but I realized Jane had no idea how awkward it was because she didn't know one of the key details. It was for this reason that I just ate the half of a hamburger Aunt Ivy handed me and didn't protest the fact that Jane was sharing all of this with her parents.

In fact, if my feelings for Jesse hadn't been in the mix, I would've been *happy* that she was telling them about it. Somehow, the more people that found out about it and didn't think I was heartless, the more confident I felt that breaking up with him was the right thing to do.

Jesse and Uncle Michael stood by the bike, finishing their hamburgers. I knew they were listening to what we were saying, but they tried to act like they weren't really paying attention.

"I feel guilty breaking up with him," I said, looking at Ivy. "If guilt wasn't a factor I would've done it a long time ago."

"She's afraid he won't make it without her, or that people will judge her," Jane said.

"I don't think either of those things are true," Ivy said.

"What are you ladies talking about?" Michael asked, looking suddenly protective as he tuned into the conversation.

"Nothing," Jane said. "If you haven't already heard what we were saying, then don't worry about it. All you would do is get bent out of shape."

"I hope nobody has hurt you," Michael said, regarding me.

"No sir," I said.

"Nope," Jane said, patting my back. "And she knows what she has to do."

I smiled and ate a handful of French fries just to mask my nervousness. Knowing what I had to do was one thing; the difficult part was doing it.

Jesse popped his knuckles, and stretched, bowing his chest like he was suddenly restless. "I'm thinking about going for a ride around the parking lot if anybody wanted to come with me," he announced, looking around as if he was genuinely seeking a passenger. As badly as I wanted to be the one to raise my hand and volunteer, I knew he was fishing for Shelby to do it, so I remained quiet. He glanced at me while he was pretending to look around the room for potential passengers, and we locked eyes for a second or two longer than I expected. I gave him a smile.

"I do, I do, I do!" Shelby yelled from Michael's arms. "I want to go on a wide awound the pawking lot!"

Jesse got onto his motorcycle, stepping over it like an expert, and looking like the hunkiest hunk I had ever seen in my whole life. I stared at him as he kick-started the engine and then smiled and wiggled his eyebrows at his niece as she giggled at the rumbling sound.

She reached for him so fervently that she nearly fell out of Michael's arms. Jesse grabbed Shelby and situated her on the seat in front of him. He held her close as he took off with her, heading out through the garage and into the parking lot. The whole routine looked like something they had done a thousand times.

"How about you?" Michael asked.

I glanced at him to find that he was looking straight at Jane. It was really fun watching Jane light up when she finally got on her new motorcycle. She had grown up in the shop and had learned to ride a long time ago, but it had been a few years, so it took her a few minutes to remember everything and work up the nerve to take off. She finally did, taking a lap around the parking lot the same way Jesse did with Shelby.

We clapped for Jane when she came back into the garage, and she stopped in front of us, waving and blowing kisses from the seat of her new ride.

"Got it?' Michael asked.

Jane beamed as she nodded.

"Are you ready to take her out and open her up?" Jesse asked.

We all knew what Jesse meant by *open her up*, and Ivy gave him a warning expression, which made us all laugh.

"We'll take Shelby over to your house," Ivy said to Jane. "I'll have your daddy drive your car so it's there when you get back. Y'all have fun. We'll give her a bath and everything."

Jane smiled and looked directly at her daughter, who was being held by her grandfather again now that she was done with her ride.

"Are you going to be okay going home with Shug and Doozy while I go for a little drive?" she asked.

"Of course she's okay," Ivy said, smiling and shaking her head at Jane for asking such a thing. "Y'all just be careful," she added. "Keep your eyes on the road, and watch for other drivers. They're not always watching for you."

Jane looked at Jesse with her eyebrows raised, and he smiled at her before focusing on me. "Are you coming?" he asked.

I didn't even answer. I just smiled and lifted the bag I was carrying. "Can you pick me up at my car?" I asked.

I hugged Michael, Ivy, and Shelby before jogging out of the garage to my car. I must've been jogging pretty quickly, or I hadn't realized how far the trek was, because I was completely out of breath by the time I made it to my car. Maybe I was just nervous. I really had to work to catch my breath as I stashed the bag into the passenger's seat. Seconds later, I turned to find that Jesse had pulled up right behind me.

"Hey," I said with a breathless smile.

"Hey," he said. He handed me a helmet and I put it on before stepping onto the back of the bike. I had ridden on the back of a motorcycle lots of times, so I wasn't timid about getting onto the seat behind him.

It wasn't until after I had already sat down, however, that I realized this time was different. The other times, I had been riding with my dad, thus I had no physical feelings or sensations whatsoever. There were definitely sensations involved this time. My whole body tingled as a result of touching Jesse.

I got on the seat behind him, putting my arms around his waist and holding onto my own hands rather than to him. I did my best to act like I wasn't going crazy with nerves and anticipation.

Chapter 14

Jesse led the way, but Jane rode right behind us and to the right where I could easily see her from over my shoulder. I tried to concentrate on her rather than the fact that my arms are wrapped around a torso of solid muscle. Try as I might to ignore it, I could feel Jesse's body through the layers of clothing, and it did nothing but make me more smitten.

The thing was, I couldn't let go. As long as I was on the back of the motorcycle, I was stuck touching him, and touching him felt way too good.

For months, I had seen the worst of Barrett, and it felt so good to feel good.

I felt free.

Being on a motorcycle helped.

I closed my eyes, and could see myself like a bird, flying through the air as the wind just rolled and whipped over me. I was lost in the moment when Jesse slowed. I opened my eyes to see that Jane had gone out front and was leading us to a gas station. Jesse pulled up beside her, parking the bike and killing the engine.

Jane smiled at us as she took off her helmet. "I should have used the restroom before we left," she said. "Can you watch it?" she asked gesturing with a flick of her chin toward the bike.

Jesse gave her a little wave, agreeing to guard it, and she smiled at him before looking at me. "Do you need to come in?"

"I don't need to use the restroom or anything, but I'll come in with you if you want."

She shook her head and stuck a hand out. "I'll be right back," she said. "Just watch my new baby."

As much as I wanted to sit there right next to Jesse on the seat, I knew I needed to create a little distance. I stood up, positioning myself next to him while he stayed sitting on the bike. He had already taken off his helmet, so I did the same, holding it with both hands in front of me.

"How have you been?" I asked since it was our first time alone in two months.

His mouth raised in a slow grin. "Fine."

"I heard you were building a house."

"Not yet," he said. "I plan to eventually, but right now I'm just buying the property."

"I heard you got yourself enough land for a little farm."

He smiled. "I don't know about that. It's three acres. It's not too far from Mom and Dad's place. I'll probably stay in the apartment and take my time building. I think I can do a lot of it myself. Dad and some of the guys at the shop will help, too."

I glanced into the store and saw that Jane had stopped to buy something. I looked at Jesse, feeling desperate to know more about him. "Are you dating anyone?" I asked. I was so nervous and awkward with my delivery of the question that he gave me an amused smile, which made me push at his shoulder.

"No, I'm not dating anyone," he said, still smiling. "You, Rose, are the one who's dating someone. I heard you were pretty serious."

"You heard me tell everyone I wish I knew how break up with him."

"I'll tell you how you break up with him," he said. "You call him, and you say, 'I want to break up'. That's how you do it." He gestured to the pay phone that was attached to the far side of the building. "There's a phone right there. All you have to do is call and say those words."

"I'm so glad you think it's that easy." I said.

Jesse wore a thoughtful expression as he looked at me, and before I knew it, he reached out, letting his fingertips brush the edge of my face. I wanted to fall into his arms, but just as quickly as he touched me, he took his fingers away. I touched my own cheek in the place where his fingers had been, feeling amazed by how much I missed his touch after only feeling it for a second.

"It *is* that easy," he said.

I glanced at the payphone, feeling crazy that I was even thinking about doing something so insane as to call Barrett and break up with him from a payphone. As I glanced in the direction of the phone, I saw Jane coming out of the convenience store. I looked at Jesse with a serious expression that said I was sorry we couldn't continue our conversation, and he just shrugged at me like he didn't see why I was upset.

"Jesse," I said.

"Rose."

"Are you serious?"

He smiled. "Yes. But if you can't do it… if you wanna stay with that guy… I'll just have to accept the rejection."

My heart fell. It felt like a piece of my chest had fallen and landed at the bottom of my gut. Jesse, the man I wanted so badly, was staring at me and saying words I had wanted to hear him say. I felt nauseous and woozy that he was bold enough to ask me to do such a thing, and terrified that I was actually thinking about it. My mind was still swimming when Jane walked up to us wearing a huge grin.

"Thank you for stopping," she said, holding out a bag of Peanut M&M's to offer them to us.

Jesse and I both politely refused without saying anything, and Jane put a handful of them in her mouth before folding up the bag and stashing them in her pocket.

"I'm ready when you are," she said.

My heart pounded. I had the distinct feeling that Jesse wanted to be with me. Somewhere deep in my heart I knew I needed to put away my doubts and fears and make that final push to do something I had been dreading for so long.

"I think I need to use the restroom," I said. "I'm sorry. I didn't think I needed to, but now that I'm standing here..." I made a regretful expression as I trailed off, handing Jesse my helmet.

I went into the store feeling like my head was swimming. For whatever reason, I thought that if I didn't break up with Barrett right then I would lose my chance with Jesse. I don't know why but something about our conversation made me feel like he had been specifically waiting for me for the last two months while I was busy being a girlfriend to someone else. I couldn't do that anymore. My heart broke just thinking about it. I was dizzy with emotion as I walked into the gas station.

"Hello!" the worker called when I came in.

"Hello," I said. It was a young guy working at the counter, and I gave him a sweet smile.

"What's your name?" I asked.

"James."

I smiled. "Hi, James, I was wondering if I could possibly use your telephone."

"There's one outside," he said.

"That's the thing," I said, nodding. "It was really nasty. I think there was gum on it. It would just be a really quick call."

James motioned for me to follow him. We went around the counter and down the short hallway to an office with a small desk. He pointed at the phone.

"You can't call long distance; it's blocked. You can call collect, though, if you press zero. All you have to do is press the button for line one and dial out."

"Thank you," I said. "I won't be long, and it's a local call."

He nodded at me, looking frustrated at the condition of the payphone. I didn't feel bad about what I said. I had glanced at it before I came inside and it was gross—the whole gas station was run-down, and I looked at the messy pile of papers on the desk, absentmindedly wondering how on earth they ever kept up with their bills in these conditions.

My thoughts jumped from one thing to another as I picked up the phone and dialed Barrett's number.

I was nauseated and terrified. I pressed the buttons stiffly, having to hang up once and start over when I thought I might have dialed the wrong number. I pushed each number carefully, numbly thinking about what I would say once he picked up.

My heart began racing when I heard the sound of the phone rustling as he picked it up.

"Hello," he said.

"Barrett, it's Rose."

"What are you doing?" he asked. "Are you coming over here?"

"I'm calling because we need to talk."

"I thought you were coming over here," he said distractedly.

"I'm not," I said. "I can't. I can't come over anymore."

He laughed. "What's that supposed to mean?"

"It means we have to break up. I'm breaking up. I think we should break up."

I stopped talking, thinking he would say something, but there was just silence on the other end.

"Hello?"

"I thought you just said you were breaking up with me."

"I did."

"Are you joking, or being serious, Rose?"

"I'm being serious. We have to do it."

"No, we don't," he said. "I can't make it without you. You're my everything, baby."

"No I'm not," I said. "I'm not that," I added, glancing at the door and trying to be quiet so that the people in the store didn't hear me.

"Rose, just come over so we can talk about this," he said. "Please. Don't do this to me over the phone."

He sounded so pitiful that I wanted to agree to it. I was tempted to give in and say I'd be right over, but then I remembered Jesse and the way he was waiting for me. I remembered how he said it was easy enough for me to just call Barrett and do it.

"I'm sorry, Barrett. I tried to stay long enough to help you out when you got hurt."

"Oh, so you had to make an effort," he sputtered in an offended tone. "Are you asking for a pat on the back for leaving me when I'm at my worst, Rose?"

"No, but I'm not..."

"Isn't this what they mean by for better or for worse, in sickness and in health."

"Yeah, but we're not..."

134

"For richer or for poorer..."

"Yeah, but we're not married," I said.

There was a few seconds of silence, and I glanced out of the door craning my head to make sure nobody was standing nearby.

"We need to talk this out," Barrett said.

"I can't," I said. "I, uh, we have to see each other again so we can get our things back or whatever, but seriously, Barrett. We have to go ahead and do it."

"Do what?"

"Break up."

"No, Rose."

"Yes. I have to go."

"No."

"I have to. I'm sorry. Goodbye, Barrett."

I hung up the phone so delicately that I heard the mumbled tones coming from the receiver as Barrett continued talking.

I stared wide-eyed at the phone as I let the receiver fully rest on the base, resulting in silence. I didn't even give myself time to contemplate what I had just done. I remembered that Jesse and Jane were in the parking lot waiting for me, and I took off, headed for the door.

"Thank you!" I called as I made my way out of the convenience store.

Jesse and Jane were still in the parking lot, and I smiled at the sight of them. Honestly, I felt as though the weight of the world had been lifted from my shoulders, and I had to work to contain the huge smile that threatened to cross my face. Jane and I exchanged smiles, but Jesse's expression was unreadable. I knew he had been expecting me to use the payphone, so I figured he had no idea that I had even talked to Barrett.

"Thank you for waiting," I said.

"No problem," Jane said. She glanced at Jesse with a smile. "You ready?" she asked.

He nodded, and they both started their engines. We all put on our helmets and I got onto the seat behind Jesse, situating myself.

My heart was pounding with anticipation.

I was so happy that I could finally feel excited by his touch without feeling terrible about it. I was overjoyed that I officially wasn't spoken for anymore.

"Hey," I said, facing the opposite way of Jane so she couldn't hear me.

"Hey," he returned, talking to me from over his shoulder.

"I did it," I said.

He glanced at me curiously, but then Jane got his attention. He nudged his chin at her, indicating that she could lead the way, and she took off in front of us. Jesse revved the engine, and we took off, through the parking lot and onto the street. I held onto him, and gave myself permission to appreciate how comfortable and content he made me.

"What did you say?" he asked, turning to holler at me from over his shoulder once we were on the road. I stretched upward, putting my mouth as close to the back of his ear as I could get it.

"I said I did it," I repeated in a loud voice that was meant to overpower the wind. "I used the phone in the store. I called and broke up with him."

Jesse didn't answer me with words. Instead, he gunned the engine, leaning the bike toward the left and going around Jane in a huge, swift, sweeping motion that had me feeling like I was riding a roller coaster.

I giggled with delight and held onto him tightly. I didn't know it was possible to show excitement through driving, but that's what Jesse did. I squeezed his waist as he whizzed past Jane, taking the lead, and challenging her to keep up with us.

We headed out of town on the straight, country road.

Chapter 15

Jesse took us on a drive down some smooth, straight, deserted roads so that Jane could try out her new wheels. He drove back to her house about a half-hour later, and we parked next to her in the driveway.

There were three other cars because Ivy was there with the baby, and Jane had roommates—not roommates, per se, but housemates. She lived in a house that had been broken up into three apartments. Jane and Shelby shared the biggest one on the main level. They had downstairs and upstairs neighbors, but they all had separate entrances and the people living in both places were quiet.

I glanced toward the house as we parked in the driveway, and I could see Shelby through the living room window. Jane got off of her motorcycle, but Jesse didn't follow suit. He also left his bike running, so I stayed where I was, holding onto him to steady myself.

Jane looked at her brother with a curious smile. "Are y'all coming in?"

"No," Jesse said. He glanced curiously over his shoulder at me. I meant to look at him and then look away, but I got entranced by his green eyes and stared for a second.

"Do you want to?" he asked, grinning at me.

"Want to what?" I asked.

"Go inside," he said.

I shook my head and then shifted my attention to Jane. "Congratulations on the bike," I said. "You look really good on that thing."

"Thank you," Jane said. "I'm so excited about it." She reached out and hugged her brother. "Thank you and Dad for working so hard on it."

Jesse smiled and nudged his chin at her after they hugged. "You're welcome," he said. "I'm glad you like it."

Jane hugged me and then looked at Shelby who was glued to the window, smiling and waving at us.

We all three waved back.

"Thanks again, brother," Jane said. "And thanks for taking me out on a ride."

"My pleasure, sister. That ride was the highlight of my day." He was being sweet to his sister, but deep down I hoped his enthusiasm had been directly caused by me riding with him.

"Mine too," she said, waving at us as she took off toward the house.

I hadn't talked to Jesse at all since I told him I ended things with Barrett, and I was nervous and scared to finally be alone with him.

I thought he might say something to me while we were still sitting in Jane's driveway, but he didn't. He just turned the bike around and took us back onto the street.

"Are we just not gonna talk about it?" I asked, leaning up to get closer to his ear as we drove.

He reached back and put his hand on the outside of my thigh as he turned to speak to me from over his shoulder. I stretched upward, putting my ear as close to his mouth as I could so I could catch the sound.

"We'll talk about it," he said.

His hand remained on my leg for a few seconds after he said it, and he moved his thumb a little, rubbing me gently before he finally let go and turned around. The contact felt protective, and it made me hold onto him a little tighter. I rested the side of my face on his back, feeling like the moment was honestly too good to be true. I could just hold on like this forever not ever get off the bike or have to explain feelings, or breakups or fears.

Unfortunately, the dream scenario only lasted a few minutes.

Before I knew it, we had arrived at the garage and Jesse was parking next to my car. I got off of the motorcycle, taking off my helmet and running a hand through my hair in the process. Jesse did the same, hanging both his helmet and mine from his handlebar.

He stood up and turned around to lean against the side of my car, taking me into his arms in the process. I gasped when he did it. I had never in my life experienced this level of intense pleasure.

"Jesse."

"Rose," he said.

He pulled me closer using a hand around my back. My knees got weak, and I felt a warm, rushing sensation.

"Jesse, we can't," I said.

He pulled back and stared down at me—his green eyes penetrating right down to my heart.

"I thought you said you broke up with him," he said.

"I did."

He shrugged. "And you know you've been thinking about me for the last two months, anyway," he said, casually looking at his fingernails, which made me laugh and fake-pound his chest.

"You're right, I have," I admitted.

He smiled. "I know."

"The only reason you know is because you were, too."

"I was what?" he asked.

"Thinking about it, me, whatever. I can't say words right now."

"You don't even have to say words, Rose. I can tell by the way you look at me, by the way you act, that you feel the same way I do."

I felt myself blushing, and I buried my forehead in his chest. "I do, and it scares me, Jesse."

"Why does it scare you?" he asked.

I glanced up. His face was only a few inches away from me and I sighed as I stared at it. I reached up and touched his cheek with my fingertips. I let them trail across the hollow of his cheek and onto his jaw.

"This," I said. "This scares me." I glanced at his mouth, but I dared not let my fingers touch it even though I wanted to. "You scare me," I said. "We're family, Jesse. We can't mess around with each other's feelings."

Really, I was just scared about my own feelings. As someone who had remained single through his early twenties, Jesse had been out with his fair share of girls, and as much as I wanted to give way to the romance of it all, I didn't want to end up on that list of girls whose hearts he broke.

"Surely you don't think I'm trying to mess around with your feelings," he said looking at me with a sincere expression.

He drew me. I felt physically drawn to him like there were magnets involved.

"Honestly, Jesse, I'm scared that this is wrong. I'm scared because right now I don't feel like I've ever felt before. It's too good, isn't it? It's gotta be wrong, I think." I glanced down at my own arms and chest, trying to think of a way to describe the physical sensations he caused. It was like nothing I had ever felt.

"Rose," he said, leaning down to get my attention.

Our eyes met, and I smiled. "What?"

"I know you. I know other girls, and I know you, and you're the one I want."

My heart was beating so quickly it felt more like it was buzzing. My ears were definitely buzzing. I looked around, having the sensation that we were being watched even though nobody was around.

"If only it was this easy," I said, dreading any possible awkward reactions from our family.

"It is this easy," he said.

He reached down and put his lips to mine.

He did it.

Jesse kissed me.

It was like nothing I had ever felt. His warm lips met mine, causing a whole host of things to happen inside my body. I had the feeling that I might melt away into nothingness. His mouth was exactly what I imagined it would be—warm and soft and perfect. He licked his lips before kissing me again.

The second contact caused a wave of intense desire to crash over me, and I squeezed his arms. "Jesse, promise me we're not doing something wrong," I whispered breathlessly.

Jesse pulled back, putting his hands around my face and regarding me with a sweet, contemplative expression. His hands were warm, and his stare made me feel amazingly content and secure. "Rose, baby, there's nothing to worry about. You and I do not share any blood. Your dad was adopted."

I bit my lip. "I know, but won't people think it's weird?"

He stared at me like he was genuinely confused. "Who? Who's gonna think it's weird?"

"My parents? Your parents? Jane? Everyone?"

"I don't think that's true."

"How can you be sure?" I asked.

"What do *you* think about it?" he asked. "Do you think it's weird?"

I shook my head. "No."

"Me neither," he said. "I don't think it's weird at all. In fact, if you want, I'll go inside and call my family to tell them what's going on. They're probably still at Jane's."

I leaned into him so that I could whisper near his ear. "And what exactly is going on with us, Jesse?"

He kept a gentle grip on my face as he stared at me. "What's going on is that I'm about to do something that's long overdo, Rose."

"You already did," I said, breathlessly.

He shook his head. "Not like I'm about to."

He let go of my face, bringing his hands to my back again, and I grinned as I leaned into him. I reached up and touched his cheek.

"What are you going to do?" I whispered only inches from his mouth. I had been waiting for this moment to arrive for so long that I felt as though Jesse would never do it.

Every second seemed like an eternity.

He squeezed my waist, pulling me even closer as he leaned down, making full and unapologetic contact with my mouth. There was no doubt or fear or guilt present in Jesse's kiss.

He kissed me so deeply that I went boneless in his arms, causing him to hold me tightly as he leaned against my car. He pulled back and smiled at me, and then he kissed my lips again like it was a genuinely fun thing to do.

"Guess what," he said. "I love you, Rose. And not just in the way I've always loved you." He placed a kiss on my cheek. "But in other ways, too."

I was so in love, I felt giddy with it. I stretched up and put my cheek next to his, smelling him and taking in all the emotions tied to this moment.

"Guess what?" I said into his ear.

I waited for his answer. I knew he was going to say 'what', and when he did, I was planning on telling him that I loved him too.

"There's Mom and Dad," he said. "They must've forgotten something." I turned to see that Jesse was staring over my shoulder in the direction of the street. My brain was so focused on other things that it took a second for me to realize what Jesse had said and that the truck approaching contained Ivy and Michael.

I instantly stepped away from Jesse, looking at him with a startled and somewhat terrified expression that reflected my true feelings.

He gave me a beseeching expression. "Rose," he said.

I shook my head at him, trying to play it cool since his dad's truck was getting closer and closer by the second.

I smiled—it was a rushed, cousinly, fake smile that didn't reach my eyes. I knew in my heart we weren't related, but it was impossible for me to let Aunt Ivy see me parked out in front of the shop, kissing her son.

I just couldn't let myself do it.

"Rose, it's not a big deal," Jesse said, seeing that faraway look in my eyes. "Don't worry about it; I'll talk to them."

He tried to reach out for me again, and as much as I wanted to go to him, I just couldn't.

I smiled and turned around just as Michael pulled into the lot and parked a couple of spots away. I held the smile, waving at Ivy and Michael as casually as I could. I glanced at Jesse who was still leaning against my car and looking at me like he couldn't believe I wanted to pretend nothing had happened.

Michael stepped out of the truck, but he left the driver's door open so that Ivy could talk to us from her spot in the front seat. They were both smiling and looking at Jesse and me like they thought the situation here in the parking lot was normal, so I figured they had no idea what had just been going on.

This made me breathe a little easier.

Michael went toward the shop, and Ivy shook her head, smiling at her husband. "He thought he might have left something plugged in," Ivy said, explaining why they were there.

"I always do that," I said nervously. "Well, I better go," I added with a sigh. I waved at Ivy and then turned to wave at Jesse. I tried to give him an apologetic expression, but he just looked at me like he didn't understand why it was going down this way. He attempted to reach for me one last time, and I high-fived his hand, stopping him in motion.

"Thanks so much for the ride," I said casually.

"I'm glad you stuck around, Rose!" Ivy called from the truck. "It was good seeing you, sweetheart. And thanks for what your doing for the shop. Michael's excited about it."

"I'm excited too!" I said.

I started retreating toward the driver's seat, trying my very best to make it seem like everything was on the up and up and this was just a normal goodbye.

I glanced at Jesse who rubbed his eyebrows. He turned and looked at me from over the car once I got over there. I positioned myself where his head was blocking Ivy's view of me, and I gave him a sorrowful expression. "I'm sorry."

"If you're sorry, then don't go right now." he said.

"I have to."

"Then you're not sorry."

I was sorry.

He had no idea how sorry I was.

"I am," I said as I opened my door. "I *am* sorry. I really do wish things were different, Jesse."

I started to get into the car, and as I did, I remembered what I was about to say to Jesse before they pulled up. "I know this doesn't make sense with what I'm doing right now, but I love you, too, Jesse." I said it hurriedly while I was in motion getting into the car, so I wasn't certain he heard me. Numbly, I started the engine and took off, smiling and waving but barely even looking at them as I drove away.

Chapter 16

I went straight to my parents' house when I left Bishop Motorcycles. I was delirious with heartbreak, and I just drove to their house on autopilot. It was one of those trips that you don't remember driving or how you got to your destination. I didn't even have a plan or realize what I was doing it until I walked into their house.

"Hey, Rose is here!" my oldest brother called from his spot on the couch.

"Hey J.J.," I said.

"Hey, beautiful Rose!" I heard my dad yell from the kitchen.

I headed in that direction, barely aware of the fact that Cottonball, my parents' dog, was jumping up on me and begging for attention. I didn't give any to him, and I didn't feel guilty about it, which was weird for me since I loved animals.

I went directly to the kitchen where I found my dad, sitting at the breakfast table with a post-dinner/pre-bedtime bowl of cereal.

"Where's mom?" I asked, leaning over to give him a hug before sitting next to him at the table.

"Reading, I think."

Just then, we heard a loud thud in the next room (which happened to be a garage that had been converted into a playroom).

Dad rolled his eyes. "Your brother has friends over," he said. "They're lucky your mom can't hear them."

"Dad, do you still have a key to Pa's cabin?" I asked.

He glanced me curiously. "Yeah, why?"

I shrugged. "Because I was wondering if I could use it for the night—go spend the night there."

"When?" he asked.

"Tonight."

His face contorted and he looked at the clock. "Are you talking about the lake house?" he asked.

I nodded, and he gave me a suspicious look like he thought I was in trouble or was maybe about to get into trouble.

"I broke up with Barrett," I said, knowing I had to let him in on some of my feelings. I sighed before continuing. "I just did it earlier tonight. It's been a long time coming, but I just did it a little while ago, and I feel a little overwhelmed."

The truth was I didn't feel overwhelmed by my break-up Barrett at all. I had been over him for a while, and if anything I was relieved in that regard. My eyes filled with tears as I stared at my dad. I wanted to tell him everything, and at the same time I couldn't.

Dad reached out and gave me a hug. "You sure it's not something else? You're not scared of going back to your apartment are you?"

He was being protective of me and thought my desire to leave town had to do with a fear of Barrett.

"I'm not scared," I said. "I just don't feel like going home right now. I went out to the cabin with Pa a couple of months ago, and it did me good to get out on the water and clear my head."

"Were you thinking of going up there alone?" Dad asked.

I nodded, and he tilted his head at me.

"Do you think you'd feel comfortable spending the night up there by yourself?" he asked.

I nodded again. "They have neighbors and a phone. Worst-case scenario, I can just turn around and drive back. It's not really that far."

"Are you sure you're okay?" he asked again. He reached out and rubbed my shoulder with a comforting touch that had me on the verge of spilling my guts.

"I'm fine," I said with a sigh. "I like it up there, and I think it'd be good to clear my head."

"I'm just not used to hearing you say you need to *clear your head*, Rose," Dad said, squeezing me around the shoulders.

In spite of being perhaps a little skeptical, he crossed the kitchen to dig in the junk drawer and came up with the key to the cabin.

"Do you think I need to call Pa and make sure nobody else staying there tonight?" he asked, handing me the key.

I shrugged at him, and he leaned over to dial the seven-digit number to my grandparents' house. I listened to his one-sided conversation.

"Hey, can I talk to Dad?"

(a pause)

"Hey, Dad, Rosie was gonna see if she could go out to the cabin for the night."

(a pause)

"Tonight. She won't bother anything. She just wanted to go up there for the night and turn around and come home in the morning."

(a pause)

"No, I have a key, I just wanted to make sure nobody was using or anything.

(a longer pause and a smile)

"I'll tell her. Love y'all too."

Dad shrugged at me as he hung up the phone. "He said nobody's there. You'll want to run the air conditioners, and they've been off for who knows how long, so it might take a little while to cool down the cabin. Be sure to turn on both of the window units. You'll see. There's a list of instructions on the refrigerator."

I smiled, clutching the keys in my hand and feeling so thankful that I had a place to go to get away. I was completely overwhelmed and could not imagine going back to my apartment and stepping back into my life as usual since my normal routine had been severely interrupted.

I hugged my dad, feeling so thankful that I had a perfect place to go.

"Whatcha doin' here, Rose? I didn't even hear you come in," Mom said, coming around the corner.

She already had on her bathrobe and slippers, so it felt a bit weird explaining to her that I was just heading out for a trip.

I took the next ten minutes to explain to her what had happened with Barrett and convince them that I was of completely sound mind regarding my decision to go out to the cabin. My dad reminded me to get gas on my way there, and I was glad he did because I only had about a third of a tank and I doubted that was enough.

I had clothes at my parents' house, so I simply packed a bag and left from there without going by my apartment. Maybe it was cowardly of me, but I didn't feel like listening to the messages that were no-doubt waiting for me from Barrett. I left town without even calling my roommate to let her know where I was going.

I took the key to the cabin and drove ninety miles north to the lake. It was a bit intimidating being there alone, but I didn't give myself time to think about that. Everything was really dark when I arrived, so I went around, turning on all the lights and locking myself in.

I checked the list on the fridge, doing all the right things that it said to do, like setting the air conditioner to a certain temperature and running the water in the sinks for thirty seconds straight. I noticed the neighbor's number was written on the sheet of paper, and I picked up the phone when I saw it just to make sure that I had a dial tone if I needed it.

I turned on the television and let it play a little bit louder than normal just to have some noise and light in the room with me.

I normally wouldn't have done something like this.

I normally would be too scared to go into the woods and sleep in a cabin by myself.

Tonight, on the other hand, I was capable of it because my thoughts were completely consumed with other things.

Tonight, I couldn't care less about the boogeyman or bigfoot.

I took a cold shower, and then I made a pallet on the couch. I didn't pull it out into a bed, but I did use about ten blankets from other beds so I could build a cozy nest on the couch. Mom and dad had sent some food with me, and I was happy to have it because I stuffed myself while watching TV. I ate snacks, watched television, and did my best to ignore my feelings for a few hours until I drifted off to sleep.

It was just after 5am when I woke up.

I had been sleeping soundly and had no idea where I was for the first few seconds. There were a few lights on in the cabin along with the TV, and I squinted at the clock and then at a window wondering if it was light out or dark. I blinked as it registered that the shades were drawn and I wouldn't be able to see out anyway. I glanced sleepily at the kitchen window, which wasn't completely covered and saw that it was still dark outside. I flopped my head onto the pillow, closing my eyes and trying my best to go back to sleep.

I opened my eyes again a few seconds later.

The television was tuned to some cooking show, and I squinted at it for a minute before I found the remote and turned it off.

I tried to go back to sleep, but I couldn't.

I was restless like I had been that night before I crawled into bed with Jesse.

I had flashbacks of that night and the next morning, and before I knew it, one thought led to another, and I had picked up a couple blankets and was on my way out to the dock.

I brought a flashlight and the blankets, and I headed out there, knowing morning was on its way and having every intention of greeting the sun as it came up over the water.

I didn't get to see the sunrise.

The same thing happened to me on the dock as it did that morning that I climbed in bed with Jesse. It was dark on the dock with only the sounds of water and nature. I wrapped myself in soft blankets, and I felt so comfortable that a heavy sleep crept over me.

The next time I opened my eyes, the sun was up.

It wasn't just coming up either—it was way up.

I glanced around, wondering what time it was but not caring enough to get up and find out. I took my time waking up. I was relaxed out there on the dock wrapped in those comforters, and I wanted to take a little while to enjoy my lakeside escape before I had to go back to Memphis.

I thought about Jesse constantly, and I still felt heartbroken and hopeless where that situation was concerned. I should have been able to listen to him. I should have been braver about saying something to his parents, but I just couldn't make myself do it. I told myself that regardless of what happened with Jesse I was happy I broke up with Barrett and tried to see the positive, but I was heartbroken.

I sat there in the midst of nature, thinking that if God could hold together the miracle of creation, then certainly He could hear me and help me.

I asked God why I ended up in this situation— one where I loved someone I was too afraid to have.

Then, I had a flashback of Pa telling me how much time a person could waste on guilt, and it sank into my heart that he was right.

I stayed out on the dock for what must have been an hour or so, letting that truth sink in and applying it to my current situation. I stayed there, soaking in the morning before deciding to head back to the cabin.

I made a cup of coffee and while it was still brewing, the telephone rang.

I hadn't been expecting anyone to call, so I looked at it, wondering if I should answer it or not.

"Hello," I said, figuring I needed to do even though I was a little afraid.

"Rose? Is that you?"

It was Jane's voice.

When I registered that it was a woman, I instantly thought it would be my mother, but it only took a second to realize it was Jane.

"Hey," I said, wondering why she would be the one calling.

"Are you at the cabin?"

"Yes," I said. "You just called me here."

There was a pause after that—one where I could tell she was trying to think of what to say.

"Rose do you love my brother?" her tone was serious and maybe even a little bit shaken and I did the thing no one should ever do.

I don't know why I did it.

It was like my arm just involuntarily straightened and set the phone back onto the receiver without my permission.

I hung up on Jane.

She asked me if I loved her brother, and I responded by reaching out and hanging up the phone.

I was still staring at the back of the receiver when it rang again a few seconds later, the loud sound startling me. I let it ring three times before finally deciding I had to pick up even though I didn't want to.

"Hello?"

"Why'd you hang up on me?" Jane asked.

"Because," I said. "Because you're tripping."

"Am I?"

"Yes, Jane, you're tripping me out asking questions like that."

"Do you, Rose?"

"Do I what?"

"Do you love my brother? He said you love him. Do you?"

I felt a longing in my chest and couldn't imagine responding with anything but the truth. "Of course I love him," I said.

"Like a cousin?" she asked.

I paused for a long time. "Yes," I said, finally.

"Well that's funny, because he seems to think you two are in love," she said.

She seemed almost annoyed, and my heart felt crushed as I realized this was the dreaded confrontation I have been afraid of.

"No, it's not like that," I said, feeling heartbroken at letting her down.

"So you *don't love him?*" she asked.

We sat there for several long seconds as I tried to bring myself to lie. I just couldn't do it.

"I do," I said. "I love him, Jane. I wish I could be with him. I'm trying to keep myself from it, but it's hard."

Several more seconds passed where Jane was silent on the other end, and I could tell she was considering what to say next.

"We all had a big discussion about it last night," she said.

That's the last thing I expected her to say, and my heart dropped.

"Who?"

"Our whole family. Jesse came over here after Mom and Dad had already left. He started telling me that he loves you and was going to be with you. He was thinking that I would give him my best wishes, and that wasn't quite what happened."

"What happened?"

"I wasn't sure about it, Rose. I didn't know what to think."

"I knew you would say that," I interrupted nervously.

I wanted desperately to hang up again, and it took all of my strength to hold the phone to my ear. "He said he wanted to be with you Rose, and I honestly didn't know what to think about that at first. We called our parents, and they came over so we could talk about it."

I sank my face into my hands feeling mortified. "Why are you telling me all this, Jane? Can't you see I already knew you would freak out, and that's what I am trying to get away from it? I can't believe your parents came over there to talk about it. Why did y'all do that?"

"They completely saw Jesse's way," she said. "They agreed with him. The first thing they did was remind me that you two weren't blood-related. Mom actually cried at the idea of you and Jesse. They supported him about it and said how cool it was that God gave him someone so close to home."

My heart, which had just been feeling broken was now coming back to life with restored hope.

"I'll tell you why I wasn't convinced, though, Rose," she continued, causing my heart to drop yet again. "I seriously love you both," she said. "What am I supposed to do if you date my brother and then break up, Rose? I would be so mad at both of you for that."

"I know," I said, since that was the main thing on my mind for the last two months. I felt heartbroken. I had seen and felt and tasted something so true that my heart ached over not being able to have it.

"Jesse had to promise me it wouldn't happen," she said.

I didn't quite understand what she meant by it. "What?"

"I said it's a good thing Jesse promised me everything would be all right."

"What's that mean?" I asked.

Jane paused again. "It means that if there's one person in this world I can count on to tell me the truth, it's my twin. I know him, and I can tell when he's lying and when he's telling me the truth." She took a deep breath. "He told me he's gonna be with you and that everything's gonna be all right, Rose. And I believe him. I think he really loves you."

Chapter 17

"Is it weird for you?" I asked Jane.

She took a second to consider my question.

"Yes, it's crazy, Rose. I mean, I honestly didn't know how to react. One time, I thought you two had something going on, but I wasn't sure... And then last night, I thought..." She hesitated. "I don't know. Apparently, I'm the only one in the family who didn't already know it was coming."

"Already know what was coming?" I asked.

"You and my brother."

"What do you mean? Who knew?"

"Everybody besides me knew y'all were destined or whatever," she said. "Pa had a dream when we were all babies. He saw you and Jesse all grown up, and he woke up knowing who y'all were and that you were together in that way—you know, married or whatever."

"Wait, Pa had a dream about *Jesse and me*?"

"Yes. When we were little. And I guess it moved him enough that he told my mom and your dad about it. He also told my mom the other day when you and Jesse were at the cabin that you looked similar to his dream."

It was difficult for me to take in what she was saying.

I had cold sweats and my ears started ringing.

"Hang on, hang on, hang on," I said. "How did Pa get involved in all this. Who all knows about this? Can you please back up and tell me who all knows about this?"

"Okay," she said. "Jesse came over to my house last night after some encounter he had with you and my parents at the shop where you ran off. He spilled his guts to me, and I told him I was too scared for this to happen, and he said it wasn't my choice, and that I had absolutely no input in the matter. So, I called Mom and Dad. We had a big family talk, and they told me they saw the whole thing coming since we were kids. That's when we talked about the dream. We had a long talk about it, and by the end of it all, I realized they were right. It's actually amazing and creative of God to put you and Jesse together from the start. I mean, I think back, and even as little kids, you were his girl, you know? I never thought I would hear myself saying this, but I can really see you two together, Rose. And I saw it in Jesse's eyes. There's love there. Real love. I guess that's why I'm calling. I wanted you to know you have my blessing to love my brother. Not that you need it, but you have it."

Her words caused tears to form in my eyes, and I blinked, causing one to fall to my cheek. "How'd you know where to find me?" I asked, glancing at the clock, which told me it was almost 10am.

"Mom called Pa and Nana this morning. She was so curious about that dream that she called him to ask about the details. That's when Pa told her the part about seeing you two on the fishing trip recently. Anyway, I think they ended up calling your dad, so I'm sure he knows about it now—not that he didn't already—you know, from the dream and everything."

I put a hand to my chest feeling completely stupefied. "Are you being serious?" I asked. "Are you telling me that family knows there's something going on with Jesse and me?"

"Yes, I am. Apparently, everyone else has been knowing it, and I'm the only one just finding out."

"Wait, I'm just finding out, too."

"Oh, yeah, so are you telling me you haven't been secretly crushing on my brother all these years?" she asked, teasing me.

I could hear the smile in her voice. I could not in clear conscious tell her that I had been crush-free all these years, so I remained silent, which caused her to laugh.

"My mom's got a picture of you and Jesse that was taken right about the time Pa had that dream. He was sitting next to you over by Nana's garden, and y'all were looking at each other. Mom brought it over last night when we called her."

"I don't think I've seen that picture," I said.

"Ask Jesse's for it," she said. "He's got it with him."

My heart dropped at the sound of his name.

Jesse.

Where was Jesse during this whirlwind? Would he forgive me for running away?

"What did Jesse say?" I asked, feeling desperate to know where he was and what he was thinking.

"He said he loved you and you loved him, and Mom cried about it. She's still amazed about it—joking around about Pa, and calling him 'the prophet'."

"Did I mess it up with him?" I asked. "Since I ran away when your parents drove up?"

"Jesse didn't come over here until after you did that, Rose."

"Where is he?" I asked.

"Somewhere between here and Dyersburg, I guess. I don't know what time he left."

"Dyersburg? Here? Is Jesse coming here?"

She laughed at my excitement. "Did I not tell you that already? I meant to. I thought it was one of the first things I said when I called."

"No, you didn't," I said, still holding the phone to my ear as I craned my neck to look out the window.

"Jesse's headed up there," she said.

"Do you have any idea when?" I asked.

"He's got to be getting close," Jane said. "I tried to call you every fifteen minutes for the last hour, but you never did pick up."

"I was out on the dock."

"Fishing?"

"Sleeping."

"Weird-o. You probably got ate up with mosquitoes."

I looked at my own arm. "I don't think I got a single bite," I said. I glanced at the clock again even though it gave me no frame of reference with Jesse's timing.

"I love you," I said, knowing I wanted to take a shower. "Thank you for calling."

"I love you, too," she said. "And please know that no matter what my initial reaction was, it honestly makes my heart happy to think about you with my brother."

"It makes my heart happy to think about your heart being happy," I said.

She chuckled.

"No really," I said. "You have no idea how much it means that you're being supportive about it."

"Uncle Jacob is adopted," she said. "So there's really nothing to be unsupportive of—other than I'll kill y'all if y'all ever break up."

"We won't," I assured her.

"That's what Jesse said," she said.

"I love you, Jane," I said, looking out the window again.

"I love you, too," she said.

I hung up the phone and instantly ran over to the window, making sure Jesse wasn't there yet. I didn't know whether he would be driving his truck or his motorcycle, but I didn't see either of them, so I decided to take a quick shower and freshen up. I glanced outside again once I was finished, but he still hadn't arrived.

I put on a little bit of makeup, watched some television, and before I knew it, it was an hour later, and Jesse was nowhere in sight.

I finally decided to go out onto the dock. It was, after all, the best part about being at the cabin, and I could still see and hear Jesse when he pulled up, so I figured, *why not wait for him out there?*

I walked out of the front door, headed down the path that led to the dock. I couldn't see the dock at first, but the closer I got, the more certain that I was that someone was sitting on it.

There was no doubt in my mind that it was Jesse. I could see it in the confident but relaxed way he held his shoulders.

"Heyyy!" I yelled, causing him to look at me.

It was Jesse all right, and he smiled and stood up as soon as he noticed I was on my way.

I was finally free to love him, and I felt like I was floating on air as I rushed down the embankment and onto the dock, moving as quickly as my feet would take me.

Chapter 18

I ran all the way to the dock, but I stopped once I set foot on it. Jesse was standing on the end of it with his hands in his pockets, looking at me with a gorgeous, entertained grin. My arms had been at my sides in a natural stance from when I stopped running, but I felt so overwhelmed that I balled my fist and put them right under my eyes so I could barely peer over them.

I just stood there, staring at him and feeling shaken, breathless, and shy. My fists were visibly shaking; I could see them out of my periphery even though I was focused on what was straight in front of me.

My chest rose and fell rapidly as I did my best to catch my breath behind the barriers of my own arms. My eyes blurred with tears. He was the most perfect man I could imagine—genuine and caring and funny and too physically gorgeous for me to concentrate on the other aspects any longer.

I took a slow step closer when he crossed his arms, and smirked at me, glancing at the space between us as if wondering if I was going to close the remaining distance or if he was going to have to do it himself.

I smiled and blinked, trying to clear the tears as I still hid behind my fists.

"How'd you get here?" I asked, glancing at my car out of the corner of my eyes. "How long have you been here?"

"About thirty minutes," he said. He pointed toward the neighbor's dock. "I parked right over there."

"Why didn't you tell me you were here?"

"Why are you hiding?" he asked, gesturing to my fists, which were still in front of my face.

I had almost caught my breath from running, but I still felt shaky and on edge with nervous anticipation.

I had flashbacks of the last day, remembering the ride and the kiss I shared with him. Then another thought hit me. I remembered the conversation I just had with Jane—the dream.

I thought of our family, and felt so very thankful about how they reacted to the news. My heart felt somehow more alive than it ever had. I literally had a different feeling in my chest. I stared at him, and he stared at me for several seconds before he cocked his head and crooked his finger at me. Just the sight of it had me supernaturally drawn to him. I smiled and took a slow step closer.

In my mind, this scene would play out differently. I imagined myself running down the dock feeling so full of uninhibited love that I would crash into him. We would fall off of the dock in a glorious, graceful splash, and come up in each other's arms, laughing and kissing and saying all sorts of quotable, touching things.

It didn't work out that way.

I approached Jesse cautiously because, honestly, my body would let me do nothing else. I took a step closer, and Jesse smiled at me before deciding to match my step with one of his own. We stopped when we were about a foot apart, standing in the middle of the dock.

Jesse pulled my hands down so he could see my face, and instead of letting go of them, he brought them up to his own chest. He positioned my hands where they faced his chest, and I opened my palms resting them against him. I still hadn't completely caught my breath from the run to the dock, and he was only making matters worse by touching me this way.

"You're shaking," he said.

I nodded since there was no point in denying it. The morning sun shone on the lake, and his green eyes were clear and bright. He held his hands over mine in an attempt to steady them. He only had on a thin T-shirt, and I could feel the heat emanating from the muscles of his chest. I felt his heartbeat, which seemed nice and relaxed, and did my best to get mine to match his.

My hands were on his chest, and his hands were covering mine, but that was the only place we were making contact.

"Rose, you're beautiful," he said, inspecting my face. "I was just staring at you as you ran over here, thinking, *what have I done to deserve this beautiful creature.*"

I smiled and shook my head. "Jesse, don't say stuff like that," I said.

"Why not? It's true."

"Because I'm already all torn up over here."

I slipped my hands out from under his and turned them, positioning them on my chest so he could he could feel my heartbeat.

"I'm all shook up," I said, smiling at him.

I used my eyes to trace the lines of his gorgeous face, unable to fully fathom that I was free to love him.

"I talked to my family," he said sweetly.

I nodded. "Jane called. She said she wasn't sure about it at first."

"She was the only one," he said. "Even your parents were happy about it."

"My parents?" I asked with a shocked expression. "Did you really tell my parents?"

He smiled. "I knew mom had talked to your dad, so I went by there on my way over here this morning. I just wanted to talk to him face-to-face, and make sure—"

"What'd he say?" I asked.

Jesse's smile broadened. "He asked if I had enough gas to get up here."

I grinned and latched onto the back of his hands, which were still resting on my chest. "I thought the song *Jessie's Girl* was about you," I said.

He smiled and went to the more relaxed position of holding me around the waist. This repositioning gave him the chance to step closer, and he did. I easily went into his arms.

"I thought it was about me, too," he said with a shrug. "Pa had a dream about us when we were little kids," he added.

I nodded. "Jane told me."

"She also told me you had a picture of us."

He grinned. "You're gonna love it. My mom brought it over to Jane's last night."

I pulled back to stare at him, my hands resting on his chest while his were wrapped around my back.

"Did you bring it?" I asked. "The picture."

He nodded.

"Do you have it with you at the cabin?"

He nodded again.

"Where is it?" I asked.

"In my pocket."

"Can I see it?"

He gave me a wry smile and nodded.

"Am I supposed to get it?"

He gave me one little nod that made me smile.

"Which pocket?" I asked.

He shrugged. "Figure it out."

"Is it in the back?" I asked as I reached behind him. I tentatively felt around for the seam that I thought might indicate the top of his pocket and ever so slowly began to slip my fingertips inside.

Jesse looked down at me, smiling at how hesitant I was being.

"Is it this one?" I asked.

"Put your hand in there and find out."

I knew by the way he said it that I had the correct pocket, so I did it. I slipped my hand into his jeans, easily finding the thick piece of paper I knew to be a photograph. I did it quickly, but there was no way I could avoid the feel of him. As much as I tried to only concentrate on retrieving the picture, my fingertips registered the feel of his body, and my heart buzzed with excitement because of it.

I turned over the photograph and stared down at it. I set it on Jesse's chest and regarded it from six inches away. I blinked, feeling tears form instantly.

I had never seen this picture before.

I was a little younger than him, and in the picture we seemed to be roughly three and four years old. He was sitting next to me with his arm around my shoulders and we were gazing straight at each other.

I stared at it for what must've been ten whole seconds before I blinked and slid it into my own back pocket. "I've never seen that picture before," I said.

"Mom had it," he said. "I guess they've all just been waiting on the day when this happened."

"That's unbelievable," I said smiling.

"What's unbelievable is that it took us so long."

"It did take us a long time, didn't it?" I returned, glancing at the hair that grew on his jaw, and thinking about what a man he was now. "I love this moment," I added.

"It's pretty good," he said with a smile.

"It's perfect, and to think I imagined it going completely different."

Jesse looked down at our proximity as if he was slightly offended. "What could you possibly want to do differently?"

I smiled and shrugged. "I thought I would do something brave and cool like keep running down the dock and tackle you into the water. It was really epic when I imagined it. We'd get all wet, and we would laugh and kiss and—"

I was right in the middle of talking when Jesse took me by the waist and hurled the both of us off of the deck and into the lake.

Chapter 19

One minute, I was telling Jesse I regretted not tackling him into the water, and the next, I was flying through the air.

Jesse left nothing to chance.

He cradled me to his chest and jumped into the water so strategically that (besides the shock of being hurled through the air unexpectedly and landing in water) it was actually an okay experience.

The water was chest deep, and after a few brief seconds of semi-ungraceful flailing about, I found my footing and regained my composure. I laughed and wiped the skin under my eyes, looking at my fingertips just to make sure there was no smeared makeup. All I had worn was mascara, anyway.

"You look beautiful," Jesse said, seeing me fuss over my appearance by touching my face.

I grinned at him. "You did that just now," I said, stating the obvious.

"Yep." He pulled me closer, and as I took a watery step toward him, a stick got wedged in between my sandal and my foot.

"Ew, I hate standing on pond floors," I said, shaking my foot rapidly. "There's a stick in my sandal. I'm always afraid it's a fish if something touches me, and it freaks me out. I don't mind swimming pools or even the beach, but I don't like the lake. You know, because of the sticks and leaves and stuff."

"You didn't think about the many, many lake-sticks and leaves in your fantasy, huh?" he asked, reaching out for me.

I laughed. "I didn't consider the sticks," I said.

He turned and headed for the ladder, pulling me behind him.

"We don't have to get out," I said, seeing what he was doing.

"I know we don't," he said with a smile. "But let's do it anyway. Come sit by me and dry off. Jumping in was the best part."

I gave him my hand and he pulled me toward him. He climbed the ladder and sat on the edge of the dock with the sun to his back, and I climbed up and sat right next to him.

"I'm lucky I didn't lose these things," Jesse said, taking off his leather flip-flops and setting them on the dock a few feet away.

I took off my shoes as well, even though they were plastic and didn't really need to dry.

Jesse rolled the cuffs of his jeans before sticking his feet into the water, and I did the same. I ran my fingers through my hair and adjusted my clothes. Jesse leaned back, propping himself up with his hands, and I followed suit, turning to smile at him once we both got settled. We had only been sitting there in that relaxed state for a few seconds when he sat up again.

I watched in amazement as Jesse shifted in all the right ways to shed his soaking wet T-shirt.

He twisted, and shrugged, and moved, and within seconds the T-shirt was off his body. Jesse carefully stretched the shirt onto the deck behind us and then got back into the same, leaning back, relaxed position.

He smiled at me, and I stared at him with a deadpan expression that must have reflected how stunned I was. He wasn't bulky, but he had defined muscles for sure, and I stared at them as he leaned back casually.

"You did that on purpose," I said.

I instinctually sat up a little straighter while trying not to be obvious. I unabashedly gawked at Jesse's torso for an awkwardly long amount of time before finally looking at his face.

"Jesse, this business with the abs is really, uh, distracting to me."

He gave me an amused smile. "I just ate before I came over here, too," he said, grinning and patting his own stomach.

The fact that he was touching it made me look at it again.

"You planned this. You pulled us into the water just so you could take this shirt off and show me what you have going on under here.

"Nu-uh," he said. "You *wanted* to be pulled into the water. Besides, I don't need to get all wet just to take my shirt off. I can do that in front of you anytime now that you're my girlfriend."

"It makes my stomach feel funny when you say that."

"Funny how? Like you need some Pepto, funny?"

I shook my head and put a hand on my chest. "It's my chest, too, not just my stomach. Say it again," I said concentrating.

"Say what? That you need some Pepto?" he asked, being dense on purpose.

I shook my head.

"Do you mean that I can take my shirt off any time I want in front of you, because you're my girlfriend?"

I nodded with my eyes closed. "That's the part. Say that one more time."

"The whole thing? Or just the word *girlfriend*?"

He asked that while leaning over and whispering directly into my ear, and my body seized up with sheer pleasure.

"The word, I think," I muttered, burying my face into my hand. "I think it's the word."

"You better enjoy it while it lasts," he said, "because I don't think it'll apply for very long."

My eyes popped open, and he smiled. "We'll move past the dating thing pretty quickly don't you think?" he asked reasonably.

My heart wanted to explode with sheer pleasure.

It was like the best Disney Princess, fairytale dream come true.

Something I honestly believed that I would never have was now a part of my reality.

I sat up, bringing my hands to my chest. "I feel warm inside, Jesse, like happiness is a tangible feeling, and I'm experiencing it right now." I looked him over with an almost disbelieving expression. "I honestly can't believe this is happening."

"Are you agreeing to marry me right now?" he asked.

I made a series of expressions that caused him to laugh. "Are you asking me?" I asked.

He took a second to seriously consider that question. "Yes, but I guess it's kind of unofficial," he said.

"Then unofficially I say *yes*, I guess."

Jesse stretched on the dock, shielding his eyes with the side of his hand as he squinted up at me, smiling. I was sitting next to him, so I turned and leaned over him a little bit, smiling at the sight of him staring up at me.

"I hate to put it this way, but if we do this right now, we're kind of stuck with each other." I leaned over him even more, staring at every curve of his face. "We're definitely stuck," I said.

Jesse used his other hand to block the sun from my eyes and I smiled at him for helping me see him more clearly. "Stuck for good," he added, grinning.

"Stuck like glue."

"I wish that part would start right now," he said.
"I wish you'd glue yourself to me right now."

"I'm right here," I said, nudging my leg toward him to show that I was already close enough to touch him.

He shook his head and pulled me closer—so close that I was leaning on his chest. My whole upper body was resting on his, and I asked him about three times if I was too heavy, but he assured me I wasn't and kept repositioning me so that I was resting right on him and putting a lot of my weight on his chest. He balled up his shirt and stuffed it under his head, using it as a pillow.

"I'm glad we got wet," I said, feeling thankful for the whole beautiful, soaked scene with his wet hair resting on a wet T-shirt and me staring down at him.

"Sorry about the sticks and leaves," he said.

"Please don't be sorry for a single second of this morning. I love the sticks. I wish I would've kept one for my collection."

"Do you have a stick collection?"

"No, but it could've been my first."

"I can pull you in the water again if you want. We can get another one stuck in your sandal."

I shook my head casually. "No thanks. I loved that you did it, but once was good. I like my current situation, anyway."

I glanced down at the fact that I was resting against Jesse's body, and the next thing I knew, I was overcome by the uncontrollable urge to kiss him. First, I was looking at his chest and then I shifted to stare at his face. I knew by the way he looked at me that if I kissed him he would most assuredly kiss me back.

"Jesse, guess what," I whispered.

"What?"

"I love you. I love you, and I'm glad I'm stuck with you. I want us to be stuck with each other. It's a relief to be stuck with you."

He held me securely to his chest. "I know. It is, isn't it?" he said. "I agree. Let's be stuck together forever. Starting now."

"Like this?" I asked. I glanced at our chests.

He nodded even though we both knew it was impossible to hold that pose forever.

I smiled and leaned in to kiss him.

I stopped when my mouth was right next to his and stayed there, unmoving for a few seconds.

"Why are you not kissing me right now?" he asked.

Our mouths were so close that I could feel his breath on my lips. I readjusted so I could get even closer to him, but I didn't let my mouth touch his. I wanted him to be the one to reach forward and close the gap, but he didn't. He waited for me to do it.

Finally, and with breathless anticipation, I let my mouth fall onto his. It was different being in control—his lips seemed softer and more relaxed. I tasted his mouth and kissed him gently several times before pulling back to stare at him.

"Whatchu stoppin' for?" he asked.

I leaned forward and kissed him again when he said it, and he nodded, which made me kiss him again.

He kept his head resting on the T-shirt so that I had to go to him.

I kissed him over and over, gentle kisses on his mouth and then on his cheek and jaw.

"I love you," I said into his ear.

I pulled back to regard him after what must have been five minutes of carefully administered kisses, and Jesse stared at me.

"Rose I will never love anyone else. I truly believe that God just made you for me and gave you to me. I know we lived our own lives for a little while, but I think we came together just when we were ready."

I ran my fingers through his hair, knowing in my heart that I would be doing things like that with this man for the rest of my life.

"Do you want to be together forever?" I asked.

"Yep."

"Yep," I said. "Because we're stuck."

"Like glue," he said.

"Oh no!" I said, feeling genuinely upset.

"What?"

"I wanted to frame it, too!" I said with utter disappointment as I fished the soaking wet photograph out of my pocket. "I wanted to hang it up at our fiftieth wedding anniversary."

"Oh no, I'm so sorry," Jesse said, when he realized. "Here, set it right here and we'll let it dry."

He stretched out and positioned the wet photograph on it a dry spot on the dock, putting the very edge of his sandal on it so that it wouldn't fly away.

"Mom might have another one," he said. "But we could show them the water logged one at our fiftieth anniversary and tell them this whole story. That'll be good, too."

I looked at the photo and then at Jesse. "Wouldn't it be amazing if we had this same picture when we're old?"

"Yep, it would," he said sweetly.

I leaned over so I could stare down at it. "Look how cute we were."

"You were," he said. "I was probably thinking about putting a frog down your shirt."

"No, you weren't. I can tell you loved me—even back then. Look how sweet."

"You're right," he said, "I really did. I've always known I was at home with you."

"I'm so happy," I said, since it was the truth.

He smiled. "How happy?"

"Seventeen-thousand miles happy," I said, stating a random amount to demonstrate how ultimately content I was.

He shook his head at me, looking entertained. "Don't tell me in miles," he said.

"How should I tell you, then?"

"Lips."

"Lips?" I asked, trying to imagine how you would measure anything in *lips*.

Jesse smiled at my look of confusion. "Lips," he repeated. He pointed at his own mouth. "Just put yours right here."

Chapter 20

Jesse and I got married four months later.

We wanted to have it in Memphis, but both of us liked the idea of doing it on a dock like the one at the lake house, so we tried to get the best of both worlds. We held it at a friend's house that had a pond with a dock and some beautiful property on the outskirts of Memphis.

It was truly a fairytale event.

Everyone went out of their way to make us feel like we had been born to be together—chosen to find one another.

Nana had another copy of that picture of Jesse and me, and as a wedding gift, she had an artist make a painting of it. Our family didn't just accept our decision to get married, they acted as if it was an event they had been anticipating—even Jane fell in love with the fact that we ended up together.

It was a perfect fall afternoon, and we had about a hundred people present at the wedding. Pa officiated the ceremony, and he told the story of his dream. He also spoke about finding my father on his doorstep in a broken-down, old Easter basket and how amazing it was that God could weave such a complicated, beautiful story to bring us together.

We had the ceremony by the pond, and the dinner and reception were held in and around the house. It was catered, and there was music, and some people stayed inside while others went out on the patio area. I was overwhelmed by the love and support, and I felt like I was walking on air until the moment when everything came crashing down. This happened in the form of Barrett, who crashed the party in devastating fashion.

One moment, we were having fun and talking to guests, and the next, one very wasted Barrett came into the house with two other guys.

I didn't recognize the guys he had with him, which was odd seeing as how Barrett and I had been together for over a year, and I knew all of his friends.

Barrett came in making a speech while the two others went directly to the table and started eating straight from it without bothering to get a plate. There was palpable tension in the room, and all of the men present stood on edge like they were ready to tackle the intruders if necessary.

Jesse was standing right next to me when Barrett started causing a scene, and I reached out and held onto his arm. He strained against my grasp, but I knew he could easily get away if he wanted.

Jesse was six feet tall with broad shoulders, but Barrett was a giant—absolutely huge. I could see the scary, empty carelessness in his eyes as he crossed the room staring straight at Jesse and me. Barrett was saying something sarcastic about not being invited to the wedding, but I couldn't really hear him because I was so dazed and out-of-it.

"Wait here," Jesse said, patting my hand.

I pulled him back to me. "What are you going to do?" I asked.

"Hit him," he said in a matter-of-fact tone.

I stared at the side of my husband's face even as Barrett continued to come toward us, still talking.

"Don't get hurt," I pleaded.

Jesse gave me a quick, reassuring smile before turning and taking a few steps toward Barrett.

They had an exchange—a heated exchange with four or five back-and-fourths, and the next thing I knew, Barrett jumped straight onto Jesse. I had been so utterly shocked that it wasn't until after Barrett made the move that I realized Jesse had invited him to do it.

What ensued was a huge fistfight.

I rushed toward them, yelling at them to stop, but my dad caught me by the arms. I strained against him, but somewhere deep inside I was glad he was holding me back. Jesse and Barrett had an extremely violent interaction with wrestling and swinging of fists, and I had no idea what I would do even if Dad let me go.

Barrett had been giving me trouble in different, more discreet ways, since we broke up, so I knew in my heart that Jesse was happy to have an excuse to hit him. They rolled and exchanged blows, and I secretly felt gratified in watching Jesse defend my honor—especially since I could tell that he had the upper hand.

Jesse got to his feet, but Barrett grabbed his ankle, trying to trip him and pull him back down. He held on for several shakes until Jesse got fed up and kicked, jabbing his foot into Barrett's side. Barrett let out a yell and released his grip enough for Jesse to regain his footing.

Barrett's friends tried to come to his defense by jumping Jesse, but other wedding guests restrained them. Barrett was a huge man and an athlete, but Jesse had the upper hand during the whole fight, so no one had tried to jump in and break it up. Jesse took a step back, daring Barrett to do any thing else, but Barrett hung his head as if he knew he'd been defeated.

I couldn't even believe what I had just seen.

A fight. There was a bloody fistfight at my own wedding—one that resulted in a table being turned over and a huge mess.

For five or ten minutes there, a real sense of panic and urgency took over the room, but just like that, it was over. My dad called his friend who was a state trooper. He came out with his lights on to reprimand Barrett and his cohorts for trespassing and destruction of property. We didn't press charges, and the whole thing was a bit of an act since the officer just came out with his lights on as a favor.

I wished it hadn't happened at all, but the only saving grace was that Jesse won the fight. He was hurt and bleeding, but he clearly won the fight.

Our reception was already wrapping up when the interruption happened, so by the time we all recovered enough to laugh about everything, it was over.

Jesse and I left the wedding site before everyone else, and they threw rice, at us before we drove off on a motorcycle with tin cans attached to it. We drove to our hotel room in downtown Memphis, which had already been set up and was waiting for us.

We stayed the night in a suite at The Peabody in downtown Memphis, and I felt like the queen of the world as I sat in the middle of the king size bed, staring at the human being I loved more than anything.

I had on white cotton pajamas. They were casual but feminine with a little lace trim. My roommate had gotten them for me, and I was glad she had because they were comfortable and cute for a bride on her wedding night.

Jesse still had on his suit from the wedding—all but the jacket and tie. He stood at the foot of the bed, slowly taking off his vest and then his thin dress shirt. He smiled at me as he dropped them on the floor. And, in the same way I did when we were out on the dock, I hid behind my own fists in sheer anticipation.

Jesse had on a tank top undershirt that was so tight and barely there I could easily see the rows of muscles underneath. He got on his knees on the end of the bed, and then slowly began to crawl toward me. His green eyes glowed, reminding me of some predatory animal. I had been so entranced by his eyes that it took me a second to catch sight of the cut—a little gash right at the top of his eyebrow, close to his temple. I followed his jawline to see some scrapes on his jaw. There was also the start of some bruising. I stared at the side of his face as he got closer and closer, finally hovering very near.

I reached out and ran my finger near the cut on his eyebrow. "Baby, you got cut," I said. "Are you sure you don't need stitches on this?"

Jesse cut his eyes to the side like he was trying to see the abrasion even though he couldn't.

Calling Jesse baby and having him act like that was normal gave me a thrill, which only intensified as he sat right next to me on the bed, pulling me into his lap. I settled in Jesse's arms, taking his face in my hands, and turning it so that I could look at his cut again.

"Is it still bleeding?" he asked. "I thought I cleaned it up."

"It's not bleeding, but it's open. Your dad looked at it, didn't he? What did he say about it needing stitches? It seems deep."

Jesse turned his head a little so I'd stop fretting over it. "Rose, you know I wouldn't trade this cut for anything, right?"

"Yeah, but I seriously might still want to see if they have some tape, Jesse. I think we could at least tape it closed."

"Rose," Jesse said, getting my attention again.

I made eye contact with him, and his mouth lifted in a slow grin. "That fight was honestly the best wedding present I could have asked for," he said, shaking his head. "Honestly, he's been running his mouth for so long that I've been praying for him to come pick a fight with me. I've actually been hitting bags and praying fervently for God to let him do something like that."

He was mostly teasing me, but he kept a straight face, which made me smile. I just held his handsome face. "I can't believe you defended my honor right there in front of everyone," I said, egging him on.

"It's unbelievable," Jesse said. "And then he went on and tried to pull me down again after I was letting him up, so I got to kick him again. It was the stuff dreams are made of."

I cracked up at that. "I'm glad you have a good outlook about it," I said. "I thought the wedding ceremony was the stuff dreams were made of, but I was thinking it went downhill during that part."

"*Went downhill?*" Jesse asked, pulling back, and looking at me with a completely serious expression. "Baby, didn't you see me out there? Right hook to the body, right hook to the face…"

I leaned back, stretching toward the bedside table where I picked up the telephone. I had to stretch with both hands to reach the receiver and press the button, and Jesse held me steady so I didn't fall off the bed.

"Who are you calling?" he asked.

"Downstairs," I explained with a whisper as the phone rang.

I was still laid out to the side, stretching toward the phone, and he smiled down at me with an amused smirk, waiting to hear what would say.

"Hello, this is Mrs. Bish—"

I had to clear my throat.

I wanted to just come out and say the name like was no big deal, but the word lodged in my throat. I felt like I wanted to cry when I said it.

"Mrs. Bishop," I finally squeaked out, squinting at Jesse and daring him to laugh at me. "Is there anyway I could get some medical tape? Or at least a bandage?" I glanced at Jesse. "My husband's got a cut. He had it before we checked in. I'd like to tape it together. Is there any way we can get a first aid kit up here?"

"Yes, ma'am. Someone will be right up to your room with that."

Five minutes later, someone brought a state-of-the-art first aid kit complete with things we would never need, like a hypothermia blanket and a snakebite kit.

I had two little brothers, so I had seen my dad make a butterfly bandage out of tape. I took my time prepping the tape and applying it to Jesse's cut so that my tiny bandage would hold the skin together perfectly.

He sat on the edge of the bed, and I stood between his legs. Jesse's arms were around me, holding me securely to him as I administered the bandage. He was looking to the side so that I could get a good view of the cut. I studied my own handiwork, thinking it would heal up nicely as long as we kept it taped like this.

I turned his face with my hands, forcing him to look right at me. I could see little piece of tape covering his cut, and it made him look tough. I smiled at him, letting my fingertips gently explore his cheeks. Because of the way he was sitting and I was standing, Jesse's head was positioned lower than mine. I leaned down and kissed him.

"That cut looks tough on you," I whispered close to his mouth.

He squeezed me.

"Have I been a good nurse, Mr. Bishop?" I whispered. "Because we here at The Peabody hotel always strive for excellence."

Jesse stared at me, unblinking for a few long seconds before he said, "This is the best day I've ever had."

Epilogue

Based on the calculations we did for increase in sales at Bishop Motorcycles and the number Uncle Michael had promised me in our initial meeting, I made over twenty-thousand-dollars on that project.

I, of course, was thankful for the experience and didn't want to take it, but Michael put that plus more toward the building of our house. My next project was a local barbeque establishment, and it went well, so we put that toward the house also.

We weren't in a hurry, so it took us nearly a year to build the house. Jesse did the contracting and we were very much a part of the project. In spite of Jesse being heir to an extremely successful company, he was a simple guy and he did a lot of the work himself or worked directly with the people he hired.

We put a lot of custom touches throughout, and by the time we moved in, it was really something we could be proud of. We built it with three bedrooms, which seemed like a ton of room, considering that we had been living in an apartment for the first year of our marriage. I had a case of nesting syndrome as we finished, though, and we worked more quickly toward the end.

Our first child was born two weeks after we moved into the house. We had a boy, and we named him Daniel after Pa. Children numbers two and three (both boys, Owen and Wesley) were born within the next three years.

Jesse and I felt blessed to have a healthy, young family with three strapping Bishop boys.

We didn't plan on having any more.

Child number four came along three-and-a-half years after Wes was born.

This one wasn't planned.

She was an unexpected gift, and we named her Ivy Alice after her grandmothers.

She was five now, and would start school soon.

I put her to bed, marveling at how quickly time just slipped through my fingers.

Jesse had just finished telling the boys 'goodnight', and he came into Ivy's room to kiss his daughter. I was standing next to her bed as he crossed the room. I watched as he leaned over, kissing her. I smiled at the sight of the muscles on the back of his arm and the fact that things like that still made my heart race.

Jesse made a big groan as he leaned over Ivy, and then a smooching sound, causing her to giggle as he kissed her neck. He pulled back to look at her, and she smiled and touched his face, near his eyebrow.

"What happened right here?" she asked.

The scar wasn't very noticeable, but Jesse liked to tease her about how he got it, and Ivy always enjoyed putting off bedtime a little bit longer by pointing it out and asking about it.

"Oh, this thing?" he asked, touching it. "I got this the night your mama and me got married."

(This was an accurate truth so far, but Jesse made a super-serious, dramatic face that Ivy and I both knew was going to be followed by some sort of outrageous lie.)

"Bandits came to our wedding. Dangerous, pirate-type guys with eye patches and swords. They tried to steal my fair bride away from me, so I had no other choice but to get in a swordfight with them. A duel to the death!" Jesse's expression was hilariously serious as he jabbed his hand through the air in a forward motion, pretending and doing a convincing job of being a fencer. "I won, of course, and the bad guys were banished to a faraway land."

"What's banished?" she asked.

"Sent away," he said.

"I'm glad they got banished and you only got this little bitty scar."

"Me too," he said.

"Did you really get it from having a fight at your wedding?" she asked, since she knew the real story and wanted to extend bedtime as much as possible.

"Yes, I did," he said, patting her head one last time. "It happened at our wedding. Only there were no swords, and it was just a regular guy, not a pirate."

"Okay," she said.

I thought she would make another comment, or ask another question about it, but she didn't. She just closed her eyes, looking content with that story.

I leaned over and kissed her one more time before Jesse and I headed out of her room and down the hall.

We peeked in on the boys and reminded them that it was time to quit talking and go to bed. The boys shared one big bedroom, and although Ivy had her own room, half the time she ended up coming into her brothers' room in the middle of the night. We had the trundle bed pulled out for her just in case. We told the boys goodnight, and headed to our room on the other side of the house.

I slid and scooted silently over the wood floors, bumping into Jesse on purpose as we walked. He smiled at me as he put his arm around me.

"I was checking you out," I whispered, still bumping into him as we moved.

"Oh yeah?"

"Uh-huh, I saw the muscles on the back of your arm a minute ago."

I reached across him and ran my fingers over the backside of his arm. I was kind of joking when I went to feel it, and I was surprised by how firm and defined his muscle was back there. I ran my fingers across the ridge of muscle, smiling at him when I noticed he was flexing for me.

"I like your muscles," I said.

And just like that, Jesse stooped in front of me and tossed me over his shoulder. The only reason I didn't let out a shriek of surprise was because I knew the kids would love an excuse to get out of their beds to come check on me. So, I stifled my squeal, holding onto Jesse and giggling silently.

He carried me the remaining feet to our bedroom and tossed me onto the bed, mumbling something about muscles before jumping up there with me.

He was my rock and my caretaker, and yet he pounced onto the bed looking silly and ferocious in an effort to make me laugh, which worked. Four kids later, and Jesse Bishop was still tickling me and making me feel like I was just falling in love.

He leaned over me and kissed my cheek, and all was right with the world.

The End
(till book 3)

Thanks to my team! Chris, Coda, Jan, Glenda

Made in the USA
Middletown, DE
06 July 2021